THE THIRTEENTH STONE OF AARON

KaCinderly Baker

Copyright © 2010 KaCinderly Baker
All rights reserved

ISBN: 149443430X
ISBN 13: 9781494434304
Library of Congress Control Number: 2013922773
CreateSpace Independent Publishing Platform
North Charleston, South Carolina

*Dedicated to
my friend Simona Hernandez Galicia,
who has enriched my life and inspired me.*

Special Thanks

*T*o *my friends whose motivation was steadfast in keeping me on track and pushing me over my writer's block*: Angela Duke, Rosa Lopez, Janet Marletto, Gracie Burkett, Dana Quintus, Donna Priester, Dawn Keith, Sharon Foster, Elizabeth Rand, Sherril McCombs, Darla Olson, Tony Hagen, Sandra Winfrey, Esther Mabry, Patricia M. Dailey, Nicole Walter, Jim Heisley, MaryAnn Scott, Cheri Baker, Danielle Coker, Harry Dierks, Andra Gibbs, Michael Baker, and Ezequiel Hinojos-Lopez.

Preface

Throughout history, religious relics have been sought after above all other artifacts. They are cherished for their perceived power to control, rule, destroy, or heal.

Rumors blended with fact have spread throughout history. This story is in relation to the softly hushed whispers of a recently discovered scroll case containing information about what is believed to be contraband from the Temple of Solomon.

The gem or crystal in this scroll case was rumored to have been taken by Alexander the Great after his conquest of Persia. After Alexander's death, the Persian priests realized the gem was not within Alexander's possessions. It was missing. This is when the Persian order it was taken from began the great search for the gem or crystal. However, its location has eluded seekers for centuries.

Prologue

New York City, twenty-first century

Rabbi Katz bid good night to his friends and walked toward the front of the synagogue, preparing to return home. While approaching the main entrance, he turned his head toward the window to admire the lovely evening. However, what he saw sent a chilling shock down his spine.

There, standing beside the streetlight, was the man—the same man who had shadowed him all day. The rabbi suspected this individual had been hired to observe and perhaps kill him.

The rabbi had discovered a religious artifact that others had spent their entire careers seeking. This artifact was so extraordinary that it was a frequent topic of discussion in archaeological circles and was desired above all other religious artifacts.

What if the stranger is a hired killer? Have I done everything necessary to secure the information and artifacts I have discovered? Second-guessing himself, he wondered whether Eli would remember their conversations and reexamine the letters he had sent, since each letter contained clues to the ancient mystery.

Fumbling within his coat pocket, the rabbi found a small matchbox that had been concealed there. Returning his attention to the hallway, the rabbi smiled and signaled for two of the synagogue's young men to come to him.

"Rabbi, what can we do for you?" they asked as they quickly approached him.

The rabbi handed them the matchbox, a small piece of paper with an address, and money and said, "Please mail this for me. I am tired and need to go home to rest. It is very important that this package be mailed tonight. God bless and keep you."

The young men took the matchbox, instructions, and money and then looked into the rabbi's face, curious about their task. Instinctively the rabbi replied, "Don't open the package, as I packed its contents very carefully and precisely. Thank you and good night."

The rabbi turned toward the synagogue's main door to exit the building. Pausing for just a moment, the rabbi took a deep breath. With the end appearing to be close, he now regretted that he had not shared more information with Eli. *Why did I not tell him about the robe and the flasks?*

As he exited the synagogue, the rabbi felt a sense of relief that the package would be sent. His first instinct was to glance again toward the streetlamp, where the ominous figure still lingered. The question foremost on his mind now was whether he would be sacrificing his life for a cause that could be won—that of protecting this special artifact. The watcher now brazenly stared directly at him , apparently unconcerned whether the rabbi or anyone else detected his presence.

Quickening his pace, the rabbi hurried down the sidewalk toward home. The watcher crossed the street and began to follow the rabbi, first accelerating and then overtaking the rabbi, grabbing him with a strong, authoritative grip.

With the sudden, overwhelming weight on his shoulder, the rabbi's heart began to pound. In a daze, time seemed to slow down, and he began to see flashes of his wife's face before him as his body uncontrollably yielded to this superior force. Paralyzed with fear, he couldn't concentrate, and the weight and strength of the vice on his shoulder caused him to stagger to the ground; the rabbi couldn't move, but he felt and heard the watcher's movements. He lay immobile as hands searched through his pockets; the rabbi's vision faded into darkness.

The Thirteenth Stone of Aaron

***

Seated comfortably in his office in the museum, Eli reviewed the latest message he had received from Rabbi Katz. It held information about a red box and accompanying crate he had sent to the museum for Eli's temporary custody and that would be delivered today. He would give him the full background on these items later, most notably three flasks in the crate and a robe in the red box. Also in the crate would be numerous essential notes, which could be mistaken for extraneous scraps of notes or newspaper clippings.

"Although I trust you with this exceptional treasure, these are extraordinary artifacts, not for display in any museum," the note explained. "Their handling requires more attention than normal archeological objects, due to certain inherent properties that cause them to affect the surrounding space-time reality. With that in mind, make certain that anyone who handles the contents of the crate is wearing the robe before opening the crate. Even that requires unusual procedures. The fabric of the robe can't be directly exposed to artificial cloth, so any polyester or other modern material must be removed." The note closed with a pleasantry. "Looking forward to seeing you and your family soon."

Eli called one of the museum's assistants, Shamar, who was setting up a display on one of the floors and asked if he would check the docks to see if two packages had arrived from New York. He gave a description of the boxes and told him that if they had arrived, to open the red box and put on the robe before opening the crate to check its contents. He added that there might be packaging material, like newspaper clippings, within the crate's box that should be retrieved and kept. Any packing material without writing could be discarded. He then emphasized the final and most important requirement that any clothing with artificial content would have to be taken off. Shamar agreed to check the dock area for the box and the crate and said when he had secured them, he would be right up.

***

Shamar, a graduate student working part time for the museum, opened the red box and gazed down at the neatly folded robe. *This is dumb*, he thought. *These archeologists have no concept of how materials react to one another.* He couldn't show up at Eli's office with his clothes under the robe though, so, glancing around to make sure no one was looking, he gave a moan, took off his clothes, and proceeded to put on the robe. He then folded his clothes and placed them tidily into the red box.

Next Shamar opened the box containing the crate. He could see the scraps of paper Eli had told him to look out for, and he placed the scraps into the robe's pockets. Just as Shamar was preparing to take the crate out of the box, three men appeared.

The one who seemed to be in charge ordered the other two, "Stop that thief, and get the crate."

Before Shamar could say anything, two thugs began to beat him severely, demanding to know why he was meddling with their property. While they were savagely attacking Shamar, the man giving the orders casually strolled over to the box containing the crate and noticed the crate had not yet been opened. Since the crate had not been tampered with, he ordered his men to stop the assault.

Woozy and suffering intense pain across his entire body, Shamar dragged himself off into a corner, hoping they would take the crate and leave him alone. He saw them pitch the red box aside and reseal the box containing the crate. All three then departed the dock with the box containing the crate.

Shamar curled into a fetal position, just wanting the pain to go away and for someone to rescue him. Grasping the robe's left pocket in his hand, Shamar attempted to wrap himself up in the robe. The room began to spin, and a very cold atmosphere began to penetrate his body. At first Shamar thought he was passing out, but because of the way the light was fading, along with the cold and accelerated spinning, Shamar thought something else could be taking place; perhaps he was dying.

CHAPTER ONE
An Unanticipated Foreigner Arrives in Alexandria, Egypt

Alexandria, Egypt, fourth century AD

The township of Rhakotis was lost from history when it was renamed Alexandria. Over time Alexandria became the home of the largest acknowledged Jewish community in the world, as well as a center of advanced learning and architectural wonders. It was renowned for its vast marble colonnades that intertwined city streets, hosting elegant white marble and stone buildings. It is a fact that on nights with full moons, one did not need streetlamps, as the marble glistened ever so bright. Its most famous structure was the great Library of Alexandria, where scholars from throughout the known world gathered for educational research and learning. Theon, the current director of the Library of Alexandria, shared his vast knowledge of mathematics and astronomy with anyone who attended his lectures. He also was a respected friend to the Roman consuls.

The heavy tolling of the midevening bell startled Theon from his reverie, reminding him that it was past time to go home. Managing the library and helping professors with their classes left him with little spare time. While hurrying down the hall toward his office, he remembered his daughter's advice to him regarding the unsafe atmosphere in the streets at night. She suggested that he leave before dark to avoid the roving bands of religious zealots that attacked any and all who challenged their beliefs. Scholars like him were prime targets.

Theon regretted losing track of time. Hastening his pace, he soon exited the halls of the library into his office. Locking his office door behind him, he pivoted and rushed to the street door on the other side of the room. Stepping across the threshold, he turned on the step to lock the door. He felt the fresh evening breeze brush against his face as he listened to the familiar click while turning the key. Uneasiness intensified throughout his body, causing hairs to rise up at the back of his neck. Anxiety rushed through his mind, warning him of danger. At the same moment, his heart began to race, and he felt like someone was watching him. With a trembling hand, he slid the key down into a pouch hanging at his side. Realizing he needed to control his nervousness, he paused and took a few deep breaths.

Theon listened intently to the night's sounds and dismissed his fears. But no sooner had he dismissed the danger from his mind than he heard the sound of approaching footsteps on the pavement behind him. He turned toward the noise, anticipating the marauders his daughter had warned him of. Theon was relieved to see Quintus, an elite guard and close friend, drawing near. In the short distance behind Quintus, Theon saw a group of his soldiers.

Quintus continued up the steps toward Theon, pausing only to bow low from the waist. He said, "Milord, we found a man lying in the road not far from here. He has been savagely beaten. When my soldiers and I reached him, well, sir, he whispered your name…"

Theon, thankful to see his friend, embraced Quintus and stepped back. Movement by the soldiers caught Theon's attention, and he no longer focused on Quintus's words. Realizing Theon seemed to hear only every other word, Quintus bowed respectfully and then stepped aside. Standing motionlessness, Quintus observed Theon's reactions to the beaten, limp body on the stretcher that his soldiers were transporting.

Theon's interest was fixed on the man lying upon the stretcher. Inquisitively Theon allowed his eyes to examine the body from head to foot. Theon's curiosity centered on the man's strange clothing; he had not seen a robe like this ever before.

From beside him Theon heard Quintus's voice enunciate firmly, "Do you know this man? Is he one of your scholars from abroad? What would you have us do with him? Shall we take him to the guest quarters or clinic?"

Theon remained silent. Walking to the injured individual, Theon gently touched his clothing. Theon felt a soft current passing through his fingertips resonating on the upper section of his hand. A strong urge to protect this individual flowed with the current traveling up his arm. A powerful but subtle curiosity about the person on the stretcher overwhelmed his senses. He didn't recognize this man or his dark, unfamiliar clothing. *Why am I enticed to assist him?* Pondering Quintus's words—*"he whispered your name"*—Theon considered his response to Quintus's question.

Quintus, still monitoring Theon's reactions, observed the expression of unfamiliarity upon Theon's face as he visually examined the body on the stretcher. This was not the response Quintus had expected to a friend or colleague. Quintus was suspicious of the foreigner's identity and unsure of what to make of Theon's reaction.

Theon struggled with how he should respond to Quintus. Perhaps it was curiosity mingled with this mysterious moment that overpowered Theon's reasoning as he blurted out, "Quintus, please bring him to my home." Theon's words echoed through the night air, returning to his ears and emphasizing his dubious decision.

The strong young guards holding the heavy stretcher heard Theon's outburst but remained still, awaiting orders from their commander. Quintus walked up to Theon to gaze deeply into his eyes.

In a deep voice of authority, Quintus asked, "Are you certain? Is this really what you want to do?"

Delaying his command to the soldiers, Quintus continued to look deeply into Theon's face. Theon seemed not only at a loss for words but also confused over his decision. Theon's face did not hide from Quintus the possibility of an uncharacteristic decision. Quintus knew Theon was hiding something from him, but what?

After waiting apprehensively for a moment, Quintus said, "I have known and respected you for many years, Theon. I find this particular situation very concerning as I don't believe you know who this foreigner is. If your decision is based on mere curiosity, I caution you that your decision may not be a judicious one."

Guiding Theon away from the stretcher and out of earshot of his soldiers, Quintus continued. "You have been a great help to me and my men for many years. Any of us would lay down our lives for you. It is only because your name was whispered to me that I brought him to you instead of the clinic. I was hoping this man, or you, could tell me who would want to injure him and why. I am prepared to make an arrest with just your word, Theon. I don't understand why you chose to have him taken to your home, but for now I will respect your request. Be aware that I and my men will be observing you as long as this foreigner is in town. I would not want to find you beaten and left in the streets."

Waiting again for Theon to say something and receiving no response, Quintus raised his arm, and with a firm, commanding voice, he spoke the order to his soldiers. "Take him to the professor's home."

The solders effortlessly glided through the streets, turning each corner with care and ensuring the least amount of discomfort to the man lying on the stretcher. It was a swift passage to Theon's home; the soldiers never slowed until they reached their destination.

Theon and Quintus followed behind the fast-paced soldiers, neither speaking. Theon was thinking about Quintus's words and contemplated why he had made this uncharacteristic decision. *I don't know this man or recognize his clothing, so what prompted me to instruct Quintus to bring him to my home? I do find myself curious about this man's circumstance as well as how he knew my name. Why did he ask for me? Why do I feel compelled to help and protect this man? Why? My instinct tells me I made the correct decision, yet Quintus's words of caution weigh heavily on my heart.*

"Where do you want my soldiers to place the man?" Quintus called out, looking to Theon for guidance.

Opening his front door, Theon entered, saying, "Please place him here," gesturing to the settee.

The soldiers gently removed the body from the stretcher and placed him on the settee. Upon completing this task, the soldiers showed their respect for Quintus by bowing and repositioning themselves just outside his front door. They stood at attention, waiting for Quintus to give further instructions.

Quintus, still sensing unease, walked through Theon's home, surveying everything with a critical eye. He began in Theon's living quarters, searching for anything out of order, and then continued through each room until he felt Theon would be safe. After inspecting Theon's home, Quintus looked toward Theon and stood before him.

Looking upon Theon's face and deep into his eyes, Quintus felt a sense of dread run through him. He asked if he could be of any further assistance or if Theon desired a guard for the night. Theon declined his offer and expressed his gratitude. Quintus looked quickly around the room once more and then upon the foreigner. Hesitantly, he bid Theon a good night. Quintus walked back out into the streets, and his soldiers followed him.

Theon listened at the door to the fading footsteps as Quintus and his guards retreated down the street. Locking the door, Theon exhaled in relief; nevertheless, he was puzzled about the man and even more baffled with himself at requesting that Quintus bring this injured foreigner to his home.

Theon moved to the settee to inspect the man's wounds so he could determine the extent of damage done to his body. He mentally noted that the man's body remained limp and his breathing was shallow. Bending on his knees at the man's side, Theon began to examine his wounds while frequently checking the man's face for movement. Theon thought he saw the man's lips moving, so he positioned himself closer to the man's face. This closer examination of the man's face revealed his lips were indeed moving ever so slightly, as if murmuring a prayer.

Theon whispered questions to the injured man, not expecting an answer. "Who did this to you? Who are you? Where are you from?"

The man, acknowledging Theon's words, viewed Theon's face through his swollen almond-shaped eyes. Theon felt compelled to listen. Placing his arm above the man's head and his ear just above the injured man's lips, Theon attempted to catch as much as he could of what was uttered. Theon rose from a kneeling position to a standing position and stared down at the foreigner, intrigued by what he had heard.

The man's brief utterance perplexed Theon; perhaps he had misheard. Theon paused for several moments, deep in thought about the foreigner's words. More importantly, he speculated whether he should do as the foreigner requested. After a long, concentrated look upon the foreigner's face, Theon concluded the answer could only be revealed if he acquired a small, sharp knife and followed the injured man's instructions. Theon left the room and returned with a knife.

As instructed, Theon took a particular section of the wounded man's clothing into his hands. When Theon touched the cloth, a sweet aroma of honeysuckle lingered in the air. He noted the silky softness of the rich, dark fabric hosting delicately formed embroidery while searching for an emblem of a treasure chest. The clothing was decorated majestically with threads of a material he didn't recognize. The exotic fabric presented a unique radiance.

Theon, on finding an insignia emblem resembling an ornate chest, grasped the knife and began to carefully cut the threads around it. As the last delicate thread was snipped, a previously well-concealed miniature scroll case fell onto the floor. Wrapped around the case was a piece of parchment paper.

Picking up the case, Theon gingerly opened it. To his surprise, a beautiful crystal fell into the palm of his hand, distracting him temporarily from the scrap of parchment that fluttered to the floor. Theon was amazed to behold what looked like a miniature lotus. The crystal was the size of a small rose whose petals were softly opened. Fascinated that each petal was a remarkable color that twinkled with its own individuality, he stared in wonder at not only the craftsmanship but the extraordinary beauty he held in the palm of his hand.

Upon each petal appeared a fine inscription in which etched wording shined in the midst of a golden or silver hue. The center of the lotus was a soft, clear blue with hints of iridescent opal flakes floating around its center, twinkling.

With difficulty, he shifted his attention to the scrap on the floor. Bending down, he grasped the scrap in his hand. A mystifying sensation tingled through him, radiating slowly throughout his entire body. The writing on the parchment was penned in Aramaic. Pulling the paper closer to his eyes, he examined it.

Theon murmured, "This paper must have been written centuries ago. Could this crystal also be as old as the writing?" He looked again at the man and realized he would not be answering any questions anytime soon, as he was now in a deep sleep. Continuing to gaze upon the injured man, Theon softly said, "What circumstance of fate has brought us together, and what have I gotten myself into?"

Placing the crystal and the parchment back into the scroll case and then into his small pouch, Theon cinched the sash tighter for security. Theon's thoughts returned to the foreigner, acknowledging the need to clean his wounds and make him as comfortable as possible.

Standing beside the injured man, Theon softly whispered to him, "You must stay alive while I investigate this mystery you brought me."

Moving to the well at the corner of his room, he filled a bowl with water. Taking some small pieces of cloth, he walked back to the foreigner so he could tend to his wounds. Theon went to his sleeping quarters and came back with a nightgown. He gently removed the robe from the foreigner and dressed him in his gown. *This crystal*, he thought to himself. *What about this crystal? What compelled a foreigner to risk his life seeking me, and for what purpose?*

When Theon finished cleaning the man's wounds, he began to prepare the robe to be washed. He found several pieces of wadded paper stuffed in a hidden side pocket. He set them aside. Theon continued to inspect the robe. The robe's fabric included a barely visible sheer structure material placed over the unusual dark material. As he drew the fabric close for inspection, he noticed the candle's light, as it touched the fabric, seemed to twinkle, as if numerous fireflies had emerged and taken flight within.

Gently he spread the robe's fabric open to understand what had been sewn upon it. The lower edges of the robe had finely embroidered star designs completed with superb craftsmanship. Never before had Theon seen such skillful detailed work combining fine threads and especially delicate crystals.

As he looked closer, he was astounded to see that the body of the robe was completely covered with fine silver crystal stars outlining the constellation Draco; each crystal star had been perfectly placed on the midnight blue fabric. Scales of shimmering gray and black thread formed the dragon's main body. Nevertheless, the artistic formation of the dragon's body appeared drab in comparison to the dragon's luminous, sparkling blue eyes.

For a moment Theon thought the dragon's eyes had followed his movements. Theon's vision fell upon the emblem of a chest sewn strategically within the mural he had partly removed. The image gave the appearance that the treasure belonged to the dragon as the dragon's claw held the emblem close to his heart, as if he controlled the treasure's fate.

Theon stood motionless in awe, trying to comprehend why the constellation Draco was upon the robe. What was its meaning? It was at this time that he noticed the edging consisted not of simple stars but of various-colored Stars of David.

Speaking out loud in an astonished voice, Theon questioned, "Could the man be of a special Jewish order? Is he an astronomer? Definitely he is a man of importance among his people because he wears such an elegant robe."

Theon cleaned the robe and hung it to dry. Returning to the settee, he pulled his chair close to the foreigner. Kneeling beside the man, Theon looked for chest movement while listening for breathing. The man was still alive. His breathing was steady and not as shallow as it had been.

Theon could not stop thinking about all that had transpired. Should he risk the danger of returning to the library at this late hour to research the parchment? Perhaps he could find Quintus or one of his guards and inquire as to where they had found the injured man. Possibly something was dropped and overlooked at the place where he was found? Would the foreigner be safe in his home with him gone? He went to the kitchen to eat bread and drink tea while considering what he should do.

After finishing his meal, Theon returned to his living room. He didn't want the man to think he was a poor host, so he placed water and bread on the small table adjacent to the man before exiting his home.

Ensuring that his belt and pouch remained securely tied around his waist, Theon decided to follow through with his intention to decipher the note. His personal safety and well-being had become a secondary concern as he began a brisk walk to the library. Theon took a deep breath of the evening's fresh air and then exhaled, thinking about the parchment and its ancient writings.

Reaching his office door, Theon pulled out his key and unlocked it. He closed and locked the door and quickly scurried to a door on the opposite side of the office. This private door opened into one of the largest rooms of the great Library of Alexandria. He unlocked this door and then placed his keys back into his pouch.

Going back to his desk, he grasped the handle of his oil lamp and pushed open the office door. He confidently crossed the threshold and entered the great library. Turning the corner, he stopped at the torch upon the wall and lit his oil lamp and continued to the area where language scrolls were kept. Much of the information held in this area was about other nations. These informative scrolls were copied and made available to scholars who wished to learn of various nations' customs, languages, and cultural idiosyncrasies. These scrolls were transcribed primarily into Latin, Greek, Hebrew, and occasionally Aramaic.

Theon moved toward the area where the Jewish scrolls containing the Aramaic language were kept. Arriving at the proper chamber, he began to search for the precise scrolls he knew could assist him. After several minutes, he found two; grasping them in his hand, he headed back to his office. He glanced around; unable to shake the feeling he was being watched. He thought to himself, *Could someone be watching me, or is this my imagination straying because of what happened this evening?* Glancing around the library halls, Theon acknowledged that the corridors appeared to be empty. The only sound was the faint clicking of his shoes. Nevertheless, the silence within the corridors hung with an eerie foreboding.

Returning to his office, he immediately closed and locked the door. Theon sat down at his desk and placed the lit oil lamp on it. Retrieving the parchment from his pouch, he gently rolled it open and began to research the scrolls listed on the parchment's message and take notes.

After completing the translations, Theon sat back in his chair, stunned by what he had deciphered. Lacking confidence in his translations, he chose to again compare his findings on the Jewish scroll with those written upon the small parchment. "Is this translation complete and accurate?" he asked himself.

Theon thought he heard a faint sound coming from the library halls. Sitting up straight, he turned his head toward the direction of the sound—the library door. A dark, melodious tune was being chanted in the distance. It was coming from the previously silent library. *Who could that be, and how did they get in?* Quickly he reexamined the contents of his pouch, convincing himself that he had not lost anything, as he was the only person with a master key to the library.

He found his key still safely secured within his pouch. Just then the chanting stopped. Theon was frozen with fear. He whispered to himself, "I'm not alone!"

Should he stay safely locked in his office until morning, or should he confront the mysterious intruder? A loud pounding upon the street door startled Theon, adding to his intense fear. He was relieved to hear Quintus's familiar voice and well-enunciated words. "Theon, I must speak with you. Open this door *now*."

Theon, without hesitation, hurried to the door and unlocked it. Standing before him were Quintus and his guards. Quintus pushed Theon aside and rushed into the room. His hand was upon his sword; Quintus was prepared for battle.

While still taking a quick look around, Quintus said out loud, "What is going on with you, Theon? You look frightened. Are you all right?"

Theon meekly replied "I left something in the library. That's all."

Quintus did not believe Theon and drew in a deep breath. "Old friend, something is going on. I have known you for nearly twenty years. In that time, you have seldom taken a foreigner into your home, and for the past two seasons, neither have you walked the streets at night. Your colleague's death at the hands of roving zealots still weighs heavy in your memory. That recollection has kept you from going out at night, but tonight you risked danger; you placed your life in harm's way to come to your office. Why?"

Receiving no answer, Quintus continued. "I am worried, Theon, about you and the injured man we found lying close to the base of Pompey's Pillar. Explain to me why you took him in, and please don't try to deceive me. I believe something exists between you and the injured man, and until I understand this relationship, I will continue to keep a watchful eye on both of you. As I stated before when I left your home earlier this evening, my soldiers and I are keeping an eye on you, not to be intrusive but to protect your life.

"When I left your home this evening, I also left behind a few of my soldiers. Their orders were to watch and guard you and to let me know immediately if you or the foreigner should leave your home. As instructed, they reported to me that you left your home, returning to the library. They also checked on the injured man at your home. He was asleep on your settee. Yes, I ordered a few guards there too to watch over him. I came here as soon as my soldiers said where they followed you to. What is going on?"

Theon did not want to lie to Quintus, so he invited him to sit at his desk so he could explain to him why he took the man into his home. Theon had just begun to speak when Quintus's guards interrupted the conversation.

"Commander, there are individuals fighting in the streets. What is your will?"

Quintus looked to Theon and said in a deep, commanding voice, "We *will* talk later. Right now I need to settle a disturbance." Exiting Theon's office into the streets, Quintus and his guards rushed toward the commotion.

As Theon locked the street door and redirected his thoughts back to the parchment, he spoke aloud. "It's obvious I need to return to the Jewish chamber and find a different scroll ... the parchment referred to a unique scroll, unlike any other, but different only in subtle ways to the trained eye ... the trained eye of a linguist. This parchment's message is a mixture of Hebrew and Aramaic languages, blended with a Hebrew idiom that even I, to some extent, do not understand!

"Yes, I have to find this unique scroll the parchment refers to. The parchment suggests that the literal answers are on this odd scroll." While pacing,

Theon considered. "If I don't seek these answers now, I will always regret my failure to follow through. I need to know the answers and what this is truly about.

"Dare I return to the corridors? Will it be safe? Who and what are chanting, and will he or she harm me? Could someone else also be seeking this parchment and crystal? What dangers have I exposed myself to? What does this have to do with me anyhow? I really don't want to go back into the library to search through more scrolls. Why didn't they place this information together to make the reassembling of the facts easier to uncover?" After some thought, Theon recharged his courage to move forward by recognizing that the only way to get answers was to reenter the library.

Unlocking the door, Theon reentered the Jewish section of the library. His thoughts focused on a set of ideas: what this scroll was alleged to contain and his wish to understand who and how this mystery had existed for so long. *Who was the foreigner, and why did he seek me out?* Theon's unwavering motivation and his desire to find answers had energized his willingness to continue forward.

Cautiously he rounded the corner. The further he was from his office door, the more his confidence faded. Slowing his pace, Theon considered his situation: the mysterious chants that had taken place in these halls, the intriguing events just outside his office door as he was headed home, his taking in a foreigner, and his discovery of the small scroll case. "However," Theon whispered to himself, "my dear friend and colleague would be ashamed if I allowed someone's chanting to stop me from pursuing this mystery." The note had mentioned, in a Hebrew jargon, concealed maps. "We both loved examining maps, and discovering concealed maps fuels my desire to complete this task.

"There are so many scrolls to search through. What if I don't find it? What if someone else has already found it? What should I do with the information? Oh, my dear departed friend, Quintus is correct that I no longer walk the streets at night because I fear that the zealots will do the same to me as they did to you; however, I shall continue this quest, honoring your example of finding all the facts, however dreadful, at whatever risk."

Arriving at the appropriate section, Theon began to search through dust-covered scrolls. It took some time before he found what he was searching for, but there it was lying on a shelf. Softly he whispered, "Why have I not noticed this scroll before!" Taking hold of the special scroll, Theon felt uneasiness.

Grasping the scroll tighter, his thoughts shifted. "Who sheltered this information, and should I expose it? Who desires its contents? Clergy will certainly want it; perhaps even kings, queens, or a leader of nations, but what else makes it so sought after!"

While going over possible scenarios, Theon loosened his grasp as panic began to take control of his thought process. He was now concentrating on the melodic chanting that had resumed somewhere deep within the library. However, this time it seemed closer. He was apprehensive to the point of terror. His instincts convinced him to rescue the book and flee back to his office.

Quickening his pace through the hallway, Theon returned safely to his office. He locked the door behind him and moved to his desk, where he dropped the scroll. Gazing at his desk, Theon became conscious that some scrolls were covered with dust while others appeared fresh or just copied. Why?

With a renewed focus, he separated the dusty scrolls from the fresh. He began reading the very dusty scroll first, which he understood from translating the parchment was not just an ordinary scroll. On the contrary, it was *the* distinct decorative ledger used to conceal essential information with reference to special items Alexander the Great had sent to this library and commanded to be hidden for his review later.

Glancing quickly across his desk, Theon searched for the small pile of dusting rags his daughter had placed there for him and grabbed one. Gently he brushed the front cover, exposing brilliant ornamentation. His need to find the answers compelled him to carefully open the ledger. There was a slight quiver in his arms as he began to open the scroll. He felt the crisp pages and smelled the fresh ink, as if the information had just been penned. *How curious,* he thought, because this ledger was hundreds of years old yet appeared to have just been copied.

His eyes widened as they quickly began to scan the markings upon the ledger. Softly he whispered, "Yes, this is certainly the special scroll of hidden treasures!" Redirecting his thoughts, he made sure both doors were locked and he was secure inside his office.

Theon dropped down into his chair and began to read the ornamental ledger. Its contents referred to a secret location within the library that contained artifacts of a religious treasure taken from the Persians' treasure room by Alexander after he overthrew their ruler. Theon's heart raced, and his reading accelerated with each sentence. Before he could finish reading the ledger, Theon slapped the ledger closed. Fear was growing within him. He grabbed a rag and wiped his face. He now was aware that something evil was searching for the crystal, as well as a scroll of knowledge and a scroll of fate that were presumably hidden with the crystal. These two items were hidden from everyone because of the potential evil that could be released on mankind.

"I must hide this ledger again! However, where can I hide it?" A wave of anxiety swept through him.

His thoughts drifted between the great Library of Alexandria, Alexander the Great, the hidden ledger, and a special messenger who Alexander the Great entrusted to bring specific treasures to the Library of Alexandria and give to none other than Aristotle. "So, the rumors of a hidden stash protected by Ptolemy *were* factual. Nevertheless, how has this great secret remained hidden for so long?"

Theon had read supporting evidence yet still didn't understand why Alexander had sent *this* special crystal to be hidden within the library, as the ledger stated. If it was so dangerous, especially if discovered evil persons, why hide it in Alexandria and bring the potential danger of retribution to Alexandria?

Theon theorized that it must be because Alexander had stumbled onto secret knowledge not known to the public but understood by scholars to exist. Did Alexander have access to the scrolls? Could he have read the scrolls, and was that why he hid them in Alexandria?

Theon was learning that the known information about the crystal and scrolls had been softly whispered about between certain clergy or religious orders that were aware of the rumored abilities of the crystal scrolls and interested in their properties. Theon's question to himself was, "Where in this vast library could treasures be hidden, and how could I not know of this place? And how did the crystal get out of the library and sewn into the robe the foreigner was wearing?"

Slumping back into his chair, Theon considered. "Was Alexander aware of what he took from the Persians' treasure room? Which Persians knew Alexander had taken this particular treasure? Is it possible Alexander never realized what a magnificent artifact he had acquired?"

Theon also did not believe Alexander would send such a treasure to the library without ordering it to be hidden and guarded only by his closest and most trusted confidants. Where would the guards have stayed, and how and where did they keep watch?

Thinking about the significance of his findings, he convinced himself that indeed a mysterious crystal had arrived from the Persian treasure room, perhaps with scrolls, and was hidden somewhere within this great library. In a very low voice, he asked himself, "Might this be the same crystal the Jewish people spoke about that may have been used by King Solomon? The information I referenced alludes to this but does not state it as a fact. Am I in possession of the crystal mentioned in the ledger, along with its scroll case, and again, how did it leave the library?"

Theon's thoughts drifted to the foreigner: his unique clothing, his beaten body, his asking for Theon by name. Theon repeated to himself, "Who is this foreigner? Why is he here? And how did he know my name?"

Standing up and clasping both hands behind his back, he paced in his office with questions rapidly flowing through his mind. Glancing down at his desk, he realized these scrolls and the ledger were to some extent easy for him to find, as if someone wanted him to glean this information.

"Even more troubling," Theon said out loud as he continued his open thoughts, "who, after all these years, is looking for this crystal? Could it be the evil mentioned within the ledger? How is the foreigner attached to this mystery?"

Abruptly Theon stopped pacing; he felt an intense urge to search for the secret room. "If this room exists," he whispered to himself, "I will find my answers there." Placing the parchment back into the pouch, he gathered all the scrolls, along with the ledger, from his desk and reentered the library chamber. He began his quest to search for the secret room!

Recalling the ledger's coded directions, he moved at a fast pace through the corridors. He needed to have the answers and be gone before morning, when the students and professors arrived for classes. "Yes, I must hurry," Theon said out loud to himself.

Reaching the staircase, Theon looked down. Recognizing the niches lining the spiral staircase mentioned in the ledger, Theon took in a deep breath. As the writing accurately stated, each niche was filled with a life-sized statue of famous men of Alexandria; there were Ptolemy, Aristotle, Eratosthanes, and Dinocrates.

The Thirteenth Stone of Aaron

Grabbing a torch from the wall, he began to descend the staircase down to the midlevel, where a marble likeness of Alexander stood within its niche. Theon paused, captivated by the beauty and colors upon Alexander's statue. He had never taken notice of these features before. He hesitated, looking up and down the stairs to see if anyone was around. Seeing and hearing no one, Theon grasped the knees of the statue, pulling them forward. Jumping back, Theon was startled by the scraping sound of stone-on-stone movement. The statue began to move inward, exposing a small, dark opening. A weak, stale breeze wafted from behind the statue out into the staircase.

Theon took a small step upward, wondering, "How could I have never known of this room?"

He grabbed the side of the opened doorway while pulling forward into the dark room. He was thankful for the torch, as it provided light for him to move around safely. Holding the torch up high, he looked for evidence that he could reopen the statue's door from within this small space. There, directly in front of him, were switches on the wall. He walked toward the switches and raised the torch for better viewing. After dusting off the switches, he saw that it appeared he could open or close the door by pulling or pushing these devices. He moved the lever down and listened as the statue began to close. Slowly the only light was that of his torch, and he observed a large arched opening to his right. He flipped the switch up to see if the door would open. It did. Closing the door for the second time using the switch, Theon redirected his attention to the arched opening from the small square entrance. Moving through the arched opening, he was curious about a faint light that radiated from the far end of the tunnel that extended before him.

He noted that the illuminating light seeping into the tunnel was from an opening at the tunnel's far right side. Taking a deep breath Theon slowly, cautiously, walked toward the light. He listened for any noise or voices from the distance in front of him. While gnawing on his lower lip, Theon thought, *I sure hope this inquisitive exploration of mine is not as dangerous as the nighttime streets of Alexandria.*

He continued following the tunnel toward the light and instinctively examined the floor and sides of the tunnel, observing that great effort had been expended to carve this tunnel. Slowing his pace, he approached the opening where light filtered into the tunnel, listening more intently for any sounds. As he drifted into the room, he was overcome with wonder, surrounded by brilliant radiance from no visible source, and engulfed in a fresh, pleasant atmosphere.

The air around him seemed cooler and crisper. The cave was so bright that his torch seemed dim compared with the soft but bright, natural iridescent glow from this ever-widening chamber.

Theon still heard no sounds. He could now see that the bright light was streaming from two tall candelabra. In a softly whispered voice, Theon called out, "Who lit these candles, and where are you?" The silence remained. Theon decided to continue following the tunnel beyond this opening to see where it led and whether there might be another entrance or at least the person who had lit the candles.

Following the tunnel for only a short distance, Theon saw that the tunnel ended abruptly. Holding his torch up high, he looked for anyone else or any other openings or levers. He found none. He did see several sconces for torches upon the wall. Cautiously Theon turned around, returning to the bright cave.

Gently he placed his feet upon the marbled steps leading down into the cave. He noted the only sounds were those of his footsteps, plus the occasional spitting from his oil-soaked torch.

Examining his new surroundings, Theon was able to view his reflection everywhere, including the ceiling. The walls are smooth, precisely chiseled, highly polished white marble. This room was large enough for perhaps twenty people; however the polished stone gave the illusion of a greater, generously proportioned area. Clearly, the floor and walls had been engineered with precision, adding to its elegance. The illumination was enhanced from the candle's gentle glow.

Moving deeper within the room, Theon gently touched one of the two lit candelabra atop a five-foot-tall marble stand. The soft glow from the delicate blue candles lent a reverent mysticism to the entire area. The ambiance surrounding him felt holy. He observed that no wax dripped from the candles. The flames appeared not to be consuming the wax.

Theon, feeling unworthy, walked back up the steps, returning to the tunnel. He momentarily contemplated leaving this area. He looked down toward the tunnel's entrance to ensure no one had followed him. Leaning toward the tunnel's entrance, he listened for sounds and heard nothing.

The Thirteenth Stone of Aaron

Returning to the cave, he had a more detailed view of two simple, undecorated wooden crates that were resting upon smaller marble pedestals, which were arranged evenly between the two candelabra. There was an empty marble pedestal where a third crate might have been. Holding his torch up and glancing around the room, Theon searched inside the cave for other entrances. There appeared to be none.

Dropping his scroll and the ledger onto the smooth stone floor, Theon heard their fall echo lightly around the chamber. Theon moved to the first crate. Examining its outer craftsmanship, he was amazed to discover it was carved from acacia wood, and it lacked any decorative markings. Slowly, he opened the crate's lid.

The air was immediately permeated by an unfamiliar fragrance. He stumbled back away from the crate, suddenly dizzy and unsteady, his vision blurred, and he perceived the illusion of numerous scrolls. His body gave up the struggle of staying awake, and his vision eclipsed the light as a calm darkness overcame him.

Theon awakened, unsure of how long he had been unconscious. Slowly, he regained awareness of where he was. For several moments, he concentrated on allowing his vision to return so he could focus his efforts on the crate's contents: *scrolls*. Using his inner strength to assist him, Theon stood once again. He was determined to find answers.

Although still lightheaded, Theon was able to walk to the crate and again gaze upon the numerous scrolls. Rummaging through the scrolls, he noted that each scroll had its own distinct colored seal or symbol upon it. Feeling fain, and fearful, *Dare I open a scroll?* was his first thought. "Yes, yes. I must persevere," he said to himself.

Returning to the crate, Theon reached in. One scroll stood out; it had a seal that depicted a cinnamon-colored goblet with surrounding misty hues. The brilliant hues that encircled the scroll's wax seal enticed him to study this one first. He grasped the scroll and went to the marble steps to sit down and read it.

Without hurrying, Theon opened the exotic scroll little by little. His anxiety rose as sweat formed across his forehead. His trembling hands betrayed his fear. Slowly and respectfully, Theon began to read, totally surprised at the contents. Finishing the scroll, he returned to the crate and searched for several distinctive scrolls mentioned in the one he had just read. He found them and took them out of the crate. A strong instinct told him to place the ornate scroll back with the others. In the process of returning the unique scroll back into the crate, it evaporated in his hand. Theon gasped in surprise. He realized he had absorbed the knowledge and that it was no longer available to anyone else. He felt humbled that he was blessed with the knowledge.

Theon was anxious about what he read. "Perhaps the other scrolls will have information about the crystal, or this cave, the robed individuals, and why they exist."

Staring at the crate, and apprehensive regarding his situation, he considered what might be best for him to do. He was confident that the injured foreigner would be of help because he had read things in the evaporating scroll about persons dressed as he was. However, he had read about four such robes, decorated with a dragon, a snake, and a phoenix, and one decorated with scrolls. The properties of each robe's guardian emblem were attributed to the wearer of each of these robes. Gathering the scrolls off the floor, he placed all of them and the ornate ledger into the crate.

Taking the parchment from his pouch, he laid it gently on top of the scrolls. With a final look into the crate, he carefully lowered the lid.

Theon became conscious that he was mumbling aloud—a nervous pattern of behavior he had acquired after the violent death of his colleague in the streets of Alexandria a few seasons earlier. Lingering for a brief moment, Theon considered how his friend would embrace this challenge. He also felt as though his friend was with him, encouraging him to follow through.

With a renewed sense of purpose, Theon walked up to the next crate. He glanced toward the bare area of an empty marble pedestal; perhaps another chest might have been there too. Arriving at the third pedestal, Theon paused briefly. His head was still lightly spinning from the first crate, and he experienced a little anxiety about this crate, knowing he must be careful.

"I've come this far and would always wonder if I don't open this crate what I might have found. Perhaps it has additional information I need to understand about what has become known and what shall become apparent."

Slowly Theon extended his arms toward the crate's sides. He felt an electrical sensation shooting up through his arms that radiated through his body and exited upward above his head. Theon realized his hands had not yet touched the crate, yet a powerful feeling had overwhelmed him.

Stepping back, he halted his examination of the chest's contents. Resting and thinking for several moments, he reached out again toward the lid. Opening the chest before him, Theon gazed upon neatly folded fine silken cloths. Reaching into the chest and moving the fabric around, Theon recognized the material's texture and the fragrance that emitted from touching the fabric. It smelled the same as that upon the foreigner's robe. Below the cloth he felt an object; it was the size of a large egg.

Pulling it to the surface, he saw a white carved marble object with a pressed-in shape that was the size and shape of the crystal. Turning the object around, Theon noticed a hollow opening in its center and a second smaller opening at its middle bottom area.

Theon thought about the crystal that had been concealed within the foreigner's garment. The crystal was the appropriate size and quite possibly would fit within the hollow-shaped object. The second opening at the bottom section resembled the markings necessary to connect a top piece to a staff.

Theon felt a slight trembling return to his arms. Frightened, he placed the object back into the chest and arranged the cloth just the way he found them.

Sitting for a while on the floor, Theon recalled a particular expression written on the disappearing scroll. He recited the paragraph aloud. "I recall an experience in which I had received similar communication. Those memories haunt me due to my underestimating the opposition. Unless swifter actions are taken, the same foe who escaped his bonds eons ago will unleash everything he can upon humanity. That foe has been silent for too many years and has undoubtedly increased his abilities."

Theon's desire to speak to the foreigner was overpowering. The foreigner resembled descriptions of individuals mentioned within the old Jewish scrolls, within the ledger, and again with almost exactly the same words within the disappearing scroll. Aloud and in a matter-of-fact way, Theon said, "In fact his physical appearance is as those mentioned in the scrolls, right down to the unique clothing."

With regret, Theon prepared to leave this inner sanctum. Slowly he walked up the steps to exit into the tunnel. He stopped and looked back into the cave. "Why do I not want to leave this place?" he said softly. A lump gathered in his throat as he turned toward the cave's entrance and softly whispered, "Thank you."

At the main opening of the tunnel, Theon listened at the door for any sign of noise. Hearing nothing, he flipped the lever up and watched as the statue's form became visible.

Once out, he pushed on the statue's knees, and the door closed. Theon scurried up the stairs, returning the torch to its stand.

Instinctively he glanced down the stairs to verify that everything had returned to its proper position. Not wanting to be noticed, Theon ran back to his office.

Unease continued to spread throughout every atom of his being as his mind briskly reviewed the facts mentioned in the ornate ledger. "Have I exposed myself to the 'someone' who seeks the knowledge I have just discovered?"

A frightening feeling rushed through his body. Not wanting to be heard, he whispered to himself, "I must remain unnoticed. I must control my emotions and my muttering!"

Plotting his route back to his office, he quickened his pace. When he was approximately a foot from his office door, believing he had gone unnoticed, Theon literally jumped through the door into his office. Once inside, he closed the door and promptly locked it.

Thankful to have returned safely, Theon leaned back against the door, gazing up at the ceiling and listening to the sounds of chatter from professors passing through the hallway. Still frightened from all the previously unknown information he had just read and what he had found, Theon didn't want to be disturbed. Also, he no longer knew who could be trusted.

He continued to speculate about who else knew of the secret room, the crystal, and the scrolls. Once more he heard that melodious chant from somewhere within the library. However, this time it was not dark but a soft, sweet hymn.

"I understand the words," he stated in a surprised voice. The chant's words became comprehensible; perhaps a result of his experiences with the crates and scrolls: "A dark, twisted foe has reopened the door toward a long and difficult journey for you that will have sad endings for some and fulfillment for others."

A sudden premonition caused him to direct his eyes to the floor, allowing him to concentrate on his discoveries. Slowly he reevaluated what he had learned from the ledger and his astonishment at the findings from within the secret room that yielded distinct knowledge of the crystal. He began to recall images of individuals associated with the crystal's safekeeping, which faintly appeared and vanished within his mind while he had read the disappearing scroll. Theon remained concerned about the empty pedestal, having no idea where the missing crate might be or what it may have contained.

Speaking softly to himself, Theon asked, "Why didn't I recognize the danger of this work when I first started my research? Why did I choose to look for a secret room? Why did I allow my curiosity to be piqued when I found a scroll yielding names of who could be trusted with this secret? Was it because the top name was Aristotle?

"What has happened to me? Have I gone mad? First I hear an unintelligible chant, and now I can understand the tune, with words clearly describing danger! What or who is chanting? How and why can I now understand the words?"

Staring around his office, Theon realized that individuals, religious or not, would be willing to kill if only to acquire possession of this crystal and the two special scrolls.

The disappearing scroll referred to exceedingly evil individuals who wished to secure this crystal and the scrolls to present them to their master, who was even more malevolent and desired to control and enslave humanity.

Theon's body trembled as he realized he had stumbled across knowledge of an old mystery protected by an ancient, deadly secret organization. He knew he could only resolve the mystery presented to him by implementing and following a precise line of investigation with the foreigner. He understood, too, that his life and the fate of the foreigner had become intertwined, and each was in grave danger.

CHAPTER TWO

Patrick Orders the Crate Brought from the Museum

Black Forest, Colorado Springs, Colorado, twenty-first century

Preoccupied and irritated, Patrick rushed into his library and slammed the door behind him. In an effort to compose himself, he paced the floor, trying to analyze why Sophia would refuse him.

"I almost had her," he said out loud to himself. "If she had accepted my meeting with her, I could have charmed her into deciphering the information I'll soon have. I need her ability and insight to make it possible for me to move forward with this"—Patrick paused and considered his words—"my father's lifelong quest.

"Ohhh," Patrick shouted out loud while clenching his fists and shaking them. "I don't yet have the answers! One thing I am sure of is that I will do anything, whatever it takes, to get Sophia on board. I desperately need her."

Patrick had been unaware of his movement and realized he had walked the full length of the west wall. The west wall, like the east, was an impressive sight, because each towered to the upper limits of the ceiling with books and knickknacks.

Pausing for only a moment, Patrick thrust his arms into the bookcase, grasping books, and in a fit of rage, he shoved them off the shelf and down upon the floor. He stopped and looked over the pile on the floor. Disgusted and dejected, he stopped his tantrum.

Composing himself, he walked toward his chair, thinking about how disappointed Sago would be with him if he didn't get the answers and especially at his failure to convince Sophia to help. With this failure, he was reminded of Sago's statement: "Your father was dealt with because of his failure."

Speaking gently to himself, Patrick said, "Oh Sophia, somehow I must convince you it is worth your efforts to help me." Patrick's thoughts quickly changed from Sophia to Shamar, and his entire demeanor transformed to anger.

Patrick's voice became acidic as he said out loud and in a well-enunciated tone, "That nuisance of a boyfriend she works with is my bane right now, and I *must* find a way around him so I can sweep Sophia off her feet and get her under my control."

Patrick sat down, sinking deeply into a decadently plush chair, and began impatiently ringing the kitchen buzzer via the blue button on his table. Obsessed with this rejection, he tried to figure out why Sophia had refused to meet with him. He was not accustomed to anyone turning him down, especially women.

Staring at the two large, life-size paintings of himself hanging on each side of the large double wooden doors, he marveled how each painting captured his likeness and illustrated his striking appearance. A tall six-foot build, well-groomed black hair, clear green eyes, a slender frame, and a perfect smile were accentuated by finely tailored clothing.

"What is there about me, Sophia that you don't find appealing? I am rich and good looking. Why do you push me away? I admire and respect you, Sophia; actually, I could even love you. You are beautiful, intelligent, and graceful beyond comprehension. Your slender figure, long, sensuous black hair, and exquisite taste in clothes add to your magnificence. I've watched you over the years and hold you in high regard. Miss Sophia Daniels, you are another mystery I have yet to solve."

Staring back into the courtyard, Patrick's mind wandered, and he again pondered how upset Sago might become. He could not envision the consequences he might face for his failure. For a moment, he deliberated on why his father's quest was so important to Sago and if so, how did Sago deal with him? What was Sago really after?

The Thirteenth Stone of Aaron

In the kitchen, Addison, a kindly older gentleman who had been the family butler for decades, was accustomed to the immature impatience of the adult juvenile who was leaning on the button, but the repeated demands from the buzzer added to his annoyance. "I'm coming, I'm coming," he said while his hand grasped the small tray with sugar, cream, and napkins. He placed the serving dish upon the large tray between the liquid refreshment and afternoon snacks.

Exiting the kitchen, Addison headed toward the master's library. Glancing over the tray, he reassured himself that he had remembered everything. Addison strove to continue providing excellent service even though Patrick didn't seem to appreciate his efforts. Addison missed the days when Patrick's mother was in charge. Patrick's mother was a true English lady. Rose had a slender build, always dressing in elegant, proper attire, and greeted their guests with genuine hospitality. She took care of the house and made sure all duties were carried out in strict English fashion. Addison missed her, "Good morning" when serving breakfast. Patrick seemed to care about no one except himself. Rose had been patient, and Patrick was not, and frankly, he was a bit of a snob!

Arriving at the closed doors, Addison knocked. Stepping back, he listened for permission to enter. There was a long pause before he heard, "You may enter."

Entering the room, Addison sensed Patrick's frustration. There he sat in his chair, staring out into the courtyard. Addison recognized immediately that Patrick was in no mood to talk. Hesitantly, he approached the table. While placing the tray down, he asked, "Is there anything else I can get for you, sir?"

Glancing around the room, he saw the mess Patrick had created. Returning his attention to Patrick's face, he saw an expression of spoiled exasperation. Addison recognized that look. He knew immediately Patrick was not in full command of his emotions. Something he wanted was being withheld, which was always a volatile situation.

Patrick's astonished voice broke the silence, broadcasting amazement at his current circumstance. "I was turned down by that gorgeous, arrogant trollop. I had planned on winning her trust and getting her help in understanding my father's special project, his quest, if you will, and figuring out how I can succeed where he failed.

"She's intelligent, well-mannered, and graceful, and she is a joy to be around. She has long legs, smooth soft black hair, beautiful brown eyes, and the fragrance of an angel. She is perfection personified."

Abruptly Patrick jumped to his feet and continued his rant. Unfortunately for Addison, he was the only other person in the room, and he had to pretend as though he cared. "Oh, how I hate being in this position. She is exactly what I want. Actually, she is precisely what I need to accomplish a particularly problematic task."

Addison was confused; was Patrick displaying a personal feeling, perhaps love for this woman or love for what she could do for him? It seemed by his rambling that Patrick felt perplexed over how to proceed with this particular situation. In this moment, Addison realized Patrick had never shown fondness for any woman before, and Addison hoped that she did not have a love of her own.

Patrick then looked at Addison and realized he sounded like an ass. He abruptly stopped speaking. "Thank you. That is all for now," Patrick said, gesturing for Addison to leave.

Addison bowed and eagerly departed the library. Rushing down the long hallway, his only thought was of returning to his kitchen, away from Patrick and his passionate rants. It was there that he felt safe from harm, as Patrick's temper tantrums usually involved throwing whatever was close.

Reaching the kitchen, he opened the door and rushed to the cupboard to grab a glass. While fixing a drink, his cell rang. It was Gabriel, Patrick's go-to man. Gabriel came from a poor blue-collar family and had always struggled to survive. His father had died while he was young, and Gabriel struggled to help his mother and sister out. Of his modest income, he kept little for himself and contributed the rest to the care of his mother and sister. Patrick had met Gabriel while he was at work on a construction site, and he had sized Gabriel up as someone he could use and someone who could use his money. Gabriel's five-foot-seven height would be considered short by some people's standards, but this young man had muscles on muscles acquired through his short adult lifetime in hard labor. His dark brown hair and eyes added to his masculine physique. Addison liked Gabriel because of his strong family values and endless efforts to improve himself and his way of life. Gabriel had spoken to Addison of his concerns and dislike of Patrick's requests of him.

"Hello, Gabriel." Addison whispered into his phone, "I must warn you before you come to the mansion that Patrick's in a foul mood." Pausing for just a moment, Addison continued, "You must be careful, Gabriel. Patrick's present state of mind seems very destructive. I'm concerned about what has come over him of late. He acts peculiar and then normal. The back-and-forth actions and verbal rants concern me deeply. Please be very careful when you're around him."

Ending the call, Addison shook his head, took another swallow of his special drink, and said out loud, "That poor lady; Patrick does seem to care a great deal for her, and perhaps that is her saving grace from his illogical behavior."

***

Gabriel ended his call to Addison and started to speculate about his theft of the crate and the beating of a monk at the museum. He was ashamed for allowing his men to strike a priest, and regret was building up because he had stolen the crate not just from a museum but from the hands of a man who served God. He longed for the days when he worked hard at the construction sites and his only fear was being late for work. His fear about Patrick revolved around his out-of-control temper.

Gabriel thought about his mother's words of late to him; she did not know where he worked or what he did, but she was concerned that the money he was bringing home was far more than what he had earned at the construction site, and she confided that she was worried that drugs or loan sharks or perhaps both were involved.

She had gently taken Gabriel's hand into hers, continuing, "Gabriel, I love you and appreciate all you have done for your sister and me since your father's death. However, if you are involved with the wrong people, leave them now. Please go back to the construction site. The owner asks me often about you and assures me that if you want to come back, he always has an opening for you."

***

Patrick stared into the courtyard, taking into account its perfectly maintained trees and bushes and his father's prize-winning rose garden. Patrick was proud of his father's garden. He was thankful his father had finished his courtyard project before his death. The workmanship and quality of materials his father chose for that project still amazed him.

Patrick's eyes followed two brick paths in a geometric design that connected to a large white marble disk. These pathways were engineered to guide one's eyes either to two large trees at the southwest corner or to a park bench situated in the southeast corner. The large marble disk, located in the exact center of the courtyard had a perfect image of Pharos Lighthouse engraved upon it.

A ten-foot-tall wall towered a few feet behind the park bench. This wall was designed after an ancient Greek decorative style, displaying tiered disks cascading downward in half-moon circles, ending at ground level on each side of the bench. Every tier that jutted out from this wall contained a potted plant, and each plant displayed a different-colored floral arrangement, adding both to the beauty and fragrance surrounding this area. Solar lights lining both sides of the pathways yielded a soft, luminous impression of safety, refuge, and comfort. When relaxing within this revered space, Patrick normally felt content.

No visitor could be immune from being entranced by this beautiful courtyard. It was even more enchanting on a clear evening, when the stars would form a magnificent heavenly ceiling.

Patrick checked for a text message from Gabriel. There was nothing. Then his cell rang. It was Gabriel. Speaking softly and calmly to hide his anxiety, Patrick said, "Hello. Do you have my crate?"

There was a minor pause because Gabriel was thinking of Addison's warning, and then Gabriel answered, "Yes sir, I have the crate. Would you like me to bring it to you now?"

"Yes!" Patrick barked without hesitation, and he instructed Gabriel to come immediately to his manor house.

Excited and anxious, Patrick was recharged with anticipation. After all these years, the ability to put his father's quest behind him and move forward with his life was in his grasp. Curiosity overwhelmed him as he wondered what kind of items would be contained in the crate and what the outer crate design might look like. Oddly, the crate contained, or it was alleged to contain, artifacts whose capabilities no writer had been able to describe.

If this was the crate, his quest to finish his father's search would be complete. At last, the moment he had so desperately been waiting for had arrived. His methodical research had paid off, and fame was within his grasp. Soon he would take hold of the elusive crate and its contents.

Exiting the library, he walked down the hall way toward his study. After reaching the two large double wooden doors, he opened them and stepped down into a huge room that dwarfed him.

Everyone who had ever entered this room was astonished by the magnificent décor and the dizzying height of the ceiling that added grandeur to an already impressive room. From its architectural elegance to its more-than-modest art collection, the room was remarkable.

The floors were highly polished imported parquet. Displayed upon the center of the floor was a generous inlaid fleur-de-lis; to the right, its east wall, was a very deep and tall fireplace, so large that two people could walk into its center together without touching the sides or top or each other. Its depth was easily six or seven feet. Located just in front of the fireplace were two generously sized polar bear rugs. To the right was a large oak desk with three decorative cloth wingback chairs. One chair was at the front of the desk facing the other two chairs. The desk had been carefully inscribed by a master craftsman to display a particular symbol around the side, back, and center area.

A tall glass bookcase, which appeared to hover just above the floor, contained small books on every shelf. A dark satin doily, whose blue contrasted with the drapes, graced the center shelf. The bookcase was well polished, and each piece of glass glimmered.

Four large round candelabra hung from the ceiling, spreading a soft light throughout the room. Each candelabrum boasted alternately colored candles of white and light rose. The back of the room had two oversize plate glass doors; each door's glass section was fitted with a drape whose delicate rose color seemed to glow with a light of its own.

Patrick rushed to his desk, sat down in a plush chair, and began to fumble in his pocket. Within seconds he produced a key. Putting the key in the center drawer, he opened and grabbed several items and flung them out upon the top of his desk. Rummaging through the items, he whispered to himself, "My key, Father's journal, and a scroll. Now I need only the crystal that should be in the crate to go along with this scroll."

The excitement continued to pulse through his body as he pressed the button for the butler. Patrick shouted, "It is finally within my grasp!" while clenching his fists in a sinister manner. "The family's quest is coming to a close." Sitting back in his chair he anxiously waited for Gabriel to arrive.

Addison arrived and stated, "You rang, sir?"

"As soon as Gabriel arrives, bring him here to this room. That will be all," he barked authoritatively. Addison turned immediately and left the room.

Patrick looked intently at the doors, anticipating Gabriel's arrival. Time seemed to crawl, and Patrick was not a patient man.

Finally Gabriel arrived at Patrick's mansion. Patrick heard the polite greetings as Addison greeted Gabriel at the front door. Patrick anxiously took mental notes of their footsteps. He knew exactly where Gabriel and Addison were relative to his study. As they approached the study doors, Patrick rose; he failed to keep calm as they approached. His passion to finally bring this long quest to an end and see for himself what had been so important overwhelmed him.

When he saw the crate clutched in Gabriel's arms, Patrick's voice cracked with eagerness as he called out, gesturing as he spoke, "Gabriel, come in and bring the crate here to me. Put it here on my desk."

Gabriel was on guard, not only because of Patrick's anxious state but because of Addison's warning. Consequently he slowed down upon entering into the study. Addison said nothing; he bowed and left the room. Gabriel continued gazing all around, taking in the study's grand surroundings. Mesmerized, he lost his ability to concentrate on what he had been instructed to do, and he walked toward the desk even slower.

Patrick clapped his hands together, sending a clapping sound throughout the room. The sound was abruptly muted by his forceful, commanding voice. "Put some stride in your step. I can arrange a tour of my study later."

Patrick's sharp tone got Gabriel's attention. Quickening his pace, he dutifully placed the chest where Patrick had instructed.

Patrick's entire body shuddered with anticipation, and he appeared anxious to touch the crate. Stepping aside only slightly, Patrick allowed Gabriel to place the crate upon his desk. As soon as the crate touched the desk's surface, Patrick shoved Gabriel aside.

Startled, Gabriel became worried about his safety. With fear running through his mind, Gabriel recalled Addison's warning. *Should I quietly leave?*

Gabriel thought to himself. Patrick's demeanor added to Gabriel's discomfort, and his senses were on high alert as he watched the transformation on Patrick's face, which was nothing short of astonishing.

Slowly and cautiously, Gabriel began to move from the side of the desk to the front of the desk, keeping his eyes positioned on Patrick and planning how and where to exit this room. His instincts told him to run, but fear partially paralyzed him. He remained in shock as he watched Patrick's trembling arms extend outward to touch the crate. Patrick looked at the crate as though it were the Holy Grail. Gabriel considered the events unfolding before him. He knew this was something beyond his understanding, and now he was terrified.

"Gabriel, were there any issues I should know about?" Patrick said, breaking the silence.

"No, no, I don't think so," Gabriel said slowly and cautiously.

Withdrawing his arms from the crate, Patrick reseated himself in his large wingback chair. Redirecting his attention to Gabriel, Patrick began asking questions; his voice and appearance had changed as he calmly asked Gabriel, "Please, please have a seat and tell me everything that happened at the museum. Make sure to leave out no details, as everything is of vital importance to me."

Gabriel concentrated on what had happened at the museum. Thinking he had recalled everything, he began to answer, "I, along with two of my men, arrived at the loading docks. To our surprise, we found a monk examining the box containing the crate. There, just in front of him, was the crate. *Your crate!* It was obvious this young man had just opened the outer packaging and was beginning to retrieve the crate. There were a few small pieces of packing material mingled with scraps of newspapers scattered about the floor at his feet. He was trying to clean up after himself because we noticed him picking up the scraps of paper and placing them in his pocket." Patrick scooted to the edge of his chair and advised Gabriel to continue.

"When the monk looked up at us, he didn't run. He just smiled at us and didn't say anything. Well, my men jumped him and roughed him up a bit. I took the box from him and examined it to see if it was what you were looking for. I decided it was, and so I asked the monk if he had removed anything from the crate. He said no and that he had not even opened the crate, just the box it was shipped in." Gabriel paused.

"Making sure he hadn't forgotten to mention anything to me, my men knocked him around a bit more, you know, just questioning him. This monk never fought back and said that everything that needed to be in the crate should still be there because he didn't open it.

"I guess he just crawled away into a corner somewhere. We were preparing to leave and noticed the monk was gone. All that remained on the dock's floor was this bloody scrap of paper that I guess he had clenched in his fist. He just disappeared. We searched again for him but could not find him. We might have broken a few ribs. I gathered what packing material he did not place in his pocket along with a few scraps of newspaper that were lying about on the floor. I placed them into this plastic bag."

Patrick's senses were on the alert about the events at the dock. He asked Gabriel, "You said he was dressed as a monk. I need you to explain his clothing to me, in detail. Tell me also where he was at the dock."

Gabriel looked at Patrick and took a deep breath. With slight annoyance, he began to explain again. "He had a long robe on, like what a monk would wear, you know dark, black I think, and shiny. I'm guessing from all the spray starch, you know priestly like. He was taking the crate out of the box when we saw him. This man was interested in removing the crate from the box and cleaning up his mess off the floor rather than seeing what was inside of the crate. He never spoke another word to us."

Patrick leaned back in his chair. His mind was reeling as to how someone from a church knew about this crate. Why was the monk interested in the packing material? Why did he put that material into his pockets? Was he just being tidy?

A sense of trepidation came over him. Patrick now considered whether anyone else besides a monk was seeking the crate. *Who*, he thought, *would send the monk*? His gaze remained fixed on Gabriel's face. Patrick let his mind envision all Gabriel had described. There was a long, uncomfortable pause before Patrick spoke again.

Patrick asked again, "Tell me, Gabriel, can you describe to me the man dressed in the robe? What I am interested in is your ability to describe in more detail this man's exact garments and physical appearance. Can you describe again these things for me?"

"I sure can," replied Gabriel with little hesitation. "He was dressed like a monk. Blond hair, five foot nine, maybe five foot ten—a white guy."

The Thirteenth Stone of Aaron

Patrick gazed at Gabriel, giving the impression that he was at a loss for words. Gabriel's description was very vague. Either he didn't pay attention to detail or he was incredibly dim-witted. Taking an envelope from the desk drawer, Patrick said, "Gabriel, thank you for finding the crate. I have something extra for you and your men. You may go now. Addison will show you out."

Patrick handed the envelope to Gabriel. Gabriel immediately placed it in his upper left pocket and turned to leave. Gabriel saw Addison waiting for him at the door, and he continued toward him.

Listening as the footsteps transitioned from his study to the front door, Patrick remained still, thinking of all that had just transpired. Soon he heard the front door close, followed by Addison's retreating footsteps. Patrick grasped the plastic bag and began to examine its contents. He carefully opened each piece of paper and softly pressed out the crumples. He stacked each piece in a pile to be sorted later. Then he began to filter through each piece of paper to determine its value.

Most of the scraps were from a New York newspaper; however, one note was not from a newspaper. The little handwritten note was addressed to Mr. Eli Daniels from a Rabbi Katz in New York.

"Dear Eli, I am happy that you are to be in possession of this robe and crate. I will meet with you soon to give you my verbal explanation of these items, which have a long history. My pursuit has been fulfilled! Be aware that before you open or touch the crate, *you must be wearing the robe*! You are the one I chose because you are trustworthy, and my prayers and meditation have brought me to the conclusion that you must be the one. Over the years we have had a humble and honest relationship where we can communicate without judgment. Please allow me this indulgence in asking you for such an imposing favor. These items must never be considered for public view, and the robe must be worn only during activity relating to the crate and its contents. I have express mailed a package and further directions for you. Respectfully, Rabbi Katz."

The rabbi had sent the crate and a red box to Eli! With a slight sense of panic, Patrick turned his attention to the crate. Amazed at what he read, Patrick for the moment stopped everything. "Wear the robe before opening the crate?" He glanced over at the crate in astonishment. He began to quickly search through the other scraps to see if he had missed anything, a warning about consequences of not wearing the robe or the reason you must wear the robe. "You must be wearing the robe" was underlined and had exclamation marks around it.

Standing up, Patrick walked toward the fireplace. While deep in thought, he spoke to himself out loud. "I don't believe this is a coincidence. How long has Eli known of the crate? What has Dr. Eli Daniels learned? Why would he be searching for a crate? Does he know about the research my father and I have done thus far?"

While looking deep into the fireplace, Patrick reached up and pulled the bell cord for Addison. "I never expected or imagined that there was anyone else looking for this crate. This information suggests I have a rival." Patrick pulled out his cell and began a text to Sago; then Patrick took cell phone pictures of the scraps of paper and the contents of the letter to Eli Daniels and sent them to Sago too.

Within moments, Addison arrived, "You rang, sir?"

"Yes," replied Patrick. "Please start the fire. I have work that will keep me busy, and I will dine here tonight."

"As you wish, sir," said Addison as he went about his duty.

Patrick's mind kept returning to the dock, trying to envision what Gabriel had described. *I feel something is missing*, Patrick thought to himself. Needing to clarify his understanding of what happened at the docks; Patrick called Gabriel and asked him to describe once more the robe the young man was wearing.

Starting to take notes, Patrick hesitated. He deemed this call fruitless, as Gabriel continued with the same vague description. Patrick asked Gabriel and his men to return to the museum to see if they could find the individual they had roughed up and to get him medical attention if needed. Perhaps they could find out who he was and why he was there as well.

Patrick decided he needed more information about Rabbi Katz; in addition, he should learn why Rabbi Katz chose Eli to be the recipient of the crate and robe. *What else did the rabbi actually confide to Eli? How involved is Eli with the crate and robe? I must know these answers. After all, this is about my father's quest. I ought to speak to Eli and ask him these questions face-to-face so I can observe his reaction to my questions.*

CHAPTER THREE
Theon and Shamar Return to the Library to Do In-Depth Research.

Library of Alexandria

Making an effort to compose himself, Theon staggered toward his desk and slumped down. He began to tremble uncontrollably as he reviewed the information he had accessed. He had just read gruesome descriptions of various people who had been caught by assassins and then tortured and slowly murdered. Worse yet was the fact that those poor souls had been tortured because someone thought they had knowledge about the gem. The main objective of the executioner was to find those who not only had knowledge of the gem but also knew its actual capabilities.

These contract killers were not paid until they yielded results; sometimes the assassins became victims because they produced no results or even worse, inaccurate results. Knowledge of the gem had become a mortal liability.

Softly, Theon spoke to the air around him. "Nevertheless, *someone* has successfully kept this relic concealed and wisely separated the knowledge of its capabilities and its whereabouts so that only one specific individual could find it."

Theon contemplated the well-thought-out codes he had deciphered from the parchment that directed the way to numerous Jewish scrolls that eventually led to the ornamental ledger. Woven within this elaborate ledger were signs intermingled with symbols that could be deciphered by a well-trained linguist and cryptologist. Furthermore, a few selected symbols had been masterfully embedded within portions of some of the more arcane Jewish scrolls. These images revealed secret abilities and attributes that had been accepted as absolute fact by their authors.

Theon reflected upon his search that had resulted in finding the secret room, acacia crates, and the other well-placed scrolls that had been dispersed cleverly throughout the library. He recalled how each scroll had played a part in yielding precise directions for finding subsequent concealed documents.

Some of the most astonishing of the new revelations had come from a scroll that related names of individuals who could be trusted. The top of the list was none other than Aristotle.

Theon concluded that his apprehension had been caused by the realization that he might be on the path to receiving some divine truth. This bizarre combination of revelations and discoveries, it seemed, might have placed him in the unenviable position as the sole custodian and protector of an ancient divine artifact and its secret nature.

Abruptly a chill passed through his body, and he moved to the fireplace and began to kindle a fire. Theon could not remember ever being this cold or frightened. His hands were trembling; was it from the cold or the fear? Uncontrollable shaking overtook him, and he fumbled clumsily, trying to start the fire.

Finally gaining control of his hands, he succeeded in producing a spark and nurturing it into a glowing ember, but he was still nearly paralyzed with fear. Squatting before the hearth, he blew lightly and encouraged the flame to grow into a roaring fire. The warmth was welcome, and he did not want to move.

Anxious and concerned for his safety, he slowly stood up and then rushed to each door to reassure himself they were all still locked. "Was I followed?" he wondered. His hearing sharpened with alertness as he listened intently to all the muffled sounds of the quiet evening.

Realizing he needed to take a break, Theon grabbed his chair, pulling it close to the hearth. He positioned a small chest close to the chair and settled down, using it as a footrest. He wanted to warm up while allowing himself a few moments to digest all that had taken place before he would return home and speak with the foreigner.

In a very low voice directed toward the warm air, he whispered, "Could the foreigner be one of the exceptional individuals mentioned in the scrolls whose duty is to guard and protect the crystal gem? His physical appearance fits the descriptions I read." He then relaxed a little and allowed the warmth from the fire to calm him. Gazing into the fire, he drifted off to sleep.

Distant sounds drew him back into consciousness; he awakened, realizing some time had passed. Gazing momentarily at the pouch, he reached down and opened it. Taking the crystal out, he placed it in the palm of his hand. Theon was still amazed to behold what looked like a miniature Lotus.

Theon experienced a new sensation flowing through his body. He felt as though a burden was being lifted from within him; simultaneously he viewed a silky vapor floating softly away, dissipating into the warm air of the fireplace. He was conscious of a new sensation taking over his body.

Sliding back into his chair and assuming an erect sitting position, Theon was aware of warm tears streaming down his face and an overpowering desire to protect this crystal and the foreigner. He also felt himself giving in to a powerful desire to learn more about the crystal and to speak to the foreigner.

Feeling more energetic, he stood up and gracefully walked to his desk. Taking a small soft cloth, he wrapped the crystal respectfully before placing it into his pouch. He firmly adjusted the ties to his belt, securing the pouch and its contents.

A sense of urgency overtook him. He promptly stood before one of his bookcases and began to search for a small pouch he knew was kept somewhere near this spot. He felt around the shelf's top; it took a while, but he was successful in finding the little pouch. Opening it, he dumped the contents into his palm.

After rummaging for a moment, he found the perfect-size crystal. Removing that crystal from the others, he refilled the small pouch with the undesired crystals and carefully put the pouch back on top of the bookcase. He examined the crystal again and knew it would be the perfect substitute. Placing the substitute crystal into his large pouch beside the other crystal, he retied it.

After glancing around the room, he returned the chest and chair to their original locations and decided to accomplish a few more things before returning home.

With several small cloths, he wiped the bookshelves and all the scrolls within his bookcases and then wiped down his desk and chair. He took a tray from the lower drawer and placed it neatly upon the desk, completing the picture by adding three cups and a teapot to the tray, taking his time to arrange them just so.

He then wrote a message on a piece of paper, folded it, and placed it prominently in front of the teapot. The note read, "I'll be back." Theon turned the tray so that the message could be seen by anyone entering through the street door.

He took one last careful look around the room, ensuring that everything had been staged fittingly as he imagined it should be. Satisfied, he unlocked the door to the street.

Stepping over the threshold, Theon turned slightly with his back to the street, and he pulled the office door closed. Turning the key, he heard the familiar click of the lock and returned his key to his pouch. Hesitating for an instant, he chuckled to himself while looking at the door, wondering whether he would ever return.

The Thirteenth Stone of Aaron

The walk home seemed shorter than before. Theon did not see Quintus or any of his guards. Reaching his front door, Theon began to wonder about the foreigner's health. He didn't wonder long though, since immediately after he entered, the stranger, who had been sitting on the settee, rose and acknowledged Theon's presence. What a change! Although the stranger still appeared battered and bruised, he looked much better than when he had left him. Theon extended his hand in an offer of friendship, and the foreigner slowly and cautiously responded in kind.

"Please sit back down," Theon said to the foreigner, gesturing with his open hand toward the settee. "My name is Theon, and I am the caretaker of the Library of Alexandria. I would like to discuss how and when you were brought to my home, and I hope you will share with me how you got here, to Alexandria, Egypt, how you know of me, and what your purpose is here."

The stranger started to speak but paused to consider his words. Unable to contain himself, he gave a temperamental outburst and said, "What are you talking about? There hasn't been a Library of Alexandria for centuries. It is a relic of ancient Egypt."

Theon was perplexed. He replied, "The Library of Alexandria has been here for centuries. Ancient Egypt! This is modern Egypt. We are the center of learning for the world."

The stranger quickly interjected, "How in the world did I get to Alexandria, Egypt, and what am I doing at a library keeper's home? And what is this strange language I am speaking, and why do I speak and understand it?"

The room became silent as both men looked at each other; both men were confused.

The stranger, speaking in a somber tone, restarted the conversation. "Theon—that is how you pronounce your name, isn't it? My name is Shamar, and I am so confused. I don't recall or understand how I got here, and I don't know why I am here. I vaguely remember that as the light was fading, I was reading a note with your name on it, and then I was rapidly consumed by a force that moved at a swift pace and dumped me on the ground. Where did you say I am? And why are you dressed oddly?"

Shamar looked around the room, which resembled a museum exhibit. Was he dreaming? The last thing he remembered was taking a beating. He had been working with artifacts from Ancient Egypt just before that; could that have triggered this dream? This had to be a dream or hallucination since it was not possible that he could have gone back in time.

Theon was amazed to hear the name Shamar. "Shamar," said Theon, pausing, "A Hebrew name referring to a precious stone?" With an anxious look upon his face, Theon was not waiting for an answer as his mind recalled items within the disappearing scroll. "You and I must talk. While you rested here, I did research at the library. I was astonished at what I learned from this research, and I am very frightened, not just for myself but for you too.

"Please fill in the missing information that I lack, because the secrets I uncovered suggest that we have little time to find the answers before some evil secret organization of assassins finds us. I must know what you remember, and the first question I have is, why did you choose me? Was it just because my name appeared on a note you read?"

Observing the blank look on Shamar's face, Theon became troubled. Shamar slowly responded, "Please bear with me. I don't understand what is going on. What is the most confusing to me is this foreign language."

"You do appear to be confused," stated Theon. "I think you are hungry and you need nourishment. Let me prepare us something to eat. Please just sit here and wait a moment while I gather some food. Know that I won't harm you, for these reasons: I feel compelled to assist you as best I can. Since your arrival, I have been doing research, and I understand from that research that there have been individuals dressed such as yourself, in similar robes, who spontaneously traveled from where they were to unknown locations. I think you arrived here because of your robe." Theon realized that he remembered this from the disappearing scroll.

"I want you to accompany me to the library, where you can see for yourself the documentation I am talking about and what I believe is the answer to how you might travel back to your homeland."

Shamar shot back an incredulous remark. "I don't have a clue what research you are referring to. What you are trying to convince me of is that I have been transported here, back in time—over a thousand years back in time. As a physicist, I cannot accept this."

Theon smiled and said, "OK then, as a scientist, tell me what you observe and what you can conclude."

Shamar looked around and had no answer.

Shamar slowly stood up and attempted to follow Theon. Theon again directed Shamar to wait on the settee again; he felt firmness and repetition were necessary since Shamar's head injury seemed to be interfering with his memory and understanding. Theon stated in an authoritative and confident voice to Shamar, "You and I need nourishment, and I need answers. I am going to the kitchen to get something for both of us to eat. It is essential that I tell you what I learned at the library, and hopefully it will jog your memory so you will share with me what you can remember. Please, please, sit back down, and I will return shortly with food and drink for both of us and I *will* answer your questions."

Shamar was frustrated and confused with his situation. A slight dizziness had come over him; he thought it might have been from standing up too fast. Recalling what Theon said, he assumed his present confusion was a result of the beating or the strange apparent teleportation to ancient Egypt.

Feeling overwhelmed, he sat back down on the settee as directed. His thoughts drifted back to his adventure on the docks and the beating. He speculated whether Eli had known what the rabbi had sent to him and whether Eli was aware of the special nature of this robe he was asked to wear.

His gut was telling him that Eli had no idea what risk was involved with the crates or the robe. A slight twinge of panic struck Shamar as realized he had no way to warn Eli, Mariah, and Sophia about possible danger from the thugs at the museum's loading dock. Shamar tried to relax, but anxiety over Sophia's safety prevented that. His thoughts then drifted to Theon's statement that he had found answers after researching a piece of parchment hidden within the robe and that he needed to accompany him to the library and examine the scrolls himself.

"OK," Shamar reasoned to himself, "I'm in a fog, and nothing makes sense. I've got to pull myself together and do what I can to get control of my situation."

What Shamar absolutely comprehended was that Theon believed he knew where to find answers that would help him understand what had happened and how to overcome his present dilemma. Shamar was skeptical that he could answer Theon's questions satisfactorily, and he admittedly was unable to grasp all that Theon was trying to tell him. Still, he must find out. *How did I arrive in Egypt? Was it the robe and why?*

His thoughts again drifted back to Sophia. He wanted to hold her in his arms and talk to her about the robe and the beating at the docks. He missed the soft smell of her perfume, her gentle voice and friendly smile. *This is distracting me*, he thought. *I must concentrate on the matter at hand, or I will never see any of them again.*

Shamar could hear Theon approaching, so he sat up straight and watched Theon's movement into the living room. Feeling dizzy again as he tried to stand, Shamar wondered whether he might have a sustained a concussion.

Theon placed a tray of food on the small table in front of the settee and handed Shamar a bowl of hot broth, pouring tea for both of them. Shamar sat back down. Breaking the silence, Theon said to Shamar, "Do you remember what you said to me last night, Shamar?"

Shamar slowly replied, "No, not at all. As I stated before, I don't remember how I got here; and where exactly is *here*, Theon? Please, tell me once again what you think happened and what your research revealed."

Theon paused for a moment; he was concerned about Shamar's first question and his lack of memory about their earlier conversation. Theon wondered whether Shamar's lack of memory was due to his head injury.

Theon explained again to Shamar that his desire to know more about him and his unique clothing overcame his normally cautious nature, resulting in him asking Quintus to bring him to his home. "You should also know that Quintus didn't want me to help you because he could tell I didn't know you."

Shamar was recalling discussions in his physics class on theories and possibilities of time travel. Shamar interrupted Theon. "Excuse me. Do I understand you are saying that soldiers carried me here? What library did you say you worked at? And am I in Alexandria, Egypt?"

Exasperated and sensing uncertainty and fright from Shamar, Theon continued his explanation of what had taken place the previous night.

Shamar remained silent as he listened to Theon. Shamar didn't distrust Theon but was bewildered at what he was hearing.

Theon was pleased that Shamar was aware of the great Library of Alexandria. Theon understood Shamar was a student of higher learning and that perhaps his memory was returning. Continuing his conversation with understanding of Shamar's confusion, Theon said, "Why yes, Shamar, the great Library of Alexandria is where I work. I am so delighted that you know about Alexandria and our library. Let me refresh your memory of what transpired."

Looking at Shamar, Theon saw not just confusion but also reservations about what he was hearing. "If I am right, Shamar, the information I collected might shed light on many of your concerns and perhaps may even hold answers for you. You were beaten and sustained head and chest injuries." Pausing only momentarily, Theon continued. "Let me begin with the scroll case you had, the note attached to it, and the crystal hidden within the scroll case. I found the case under the emblem of your robe."

"Wait a minute!" Shamar interjected. "What note, what emblem, and where on what robe?"

Ignoring the outburst, Theon continued while cautiously observing Shamar and explained to him the events that had transpired the previous night. "I removed an emblem from just beneath the dragon's claw. The emblem was of a treasure chest, and sewn under that emblem was a miniature scroll case that contained a crystal with a note attached to it. I removed the note as you instructed me to, and I have deciphered it."

Shamar exclaimed, "I know nothing about this robe and zilch about a scroll case. I work at a museum in Colorado. My boss is Mr. Eli Daniels." Stopping for a moment, Shamar remembered, "Oh, oh yes, Mr. Daniels asked me to wear a robe before I picked up a crate."

Theon sat up straight, shocked to hear a crate mentioned. He considered that the missing crate might be the one that Shamar was unpacking at the museum. He felt slightly panicked as he wondered whether assassins had been to the secret room and taken the missing crate and somehow they traveled back to Shamar's homeland. With a slight trembling in his voice, Theon continued his conversation. "The note was written in Aramaic. I needed to research Jewish scrolls within the library to decipher it. One scroll led to another and so on until I had compiled information about a very dangerous religious artifact. It is not so much the artifact that is dangerous but the individuals who are trying to acquire it. Tell me, Shamar, what did the crate look like that you saw in the box?"

The Thirteenth Stone of Aaron

Not receiving an answer, Theon continued, "I have learned that this artifact is shrouded in mystery and intrigue, to include the murder and torture of many individuals, actually a lot of individuals. However, someone protected the crystal by concealing it within your robe. How did you come into possession of this robe?"

Shamar hesitated for a moment; his head was throbbing, and he still felt a little dizzy. He was considering his answer to Theon, curious whether he would understand that time travel might be involved. Shamar did not understand how or why he had become involved in this mystery. Presently he was regretting not paying more attention to the time travel discussions.

Shamar began to explain what he remembered to Theon. "I am remembering a few pieces of this puzzle. Professor Daniels was waiting for a particular crate to arrive from New York. The crate was from a friend of his, a rabbi. When the crate arrived, I was instructed to wear this robe before touching the crate. After putting on the robe, I picked up the crate, as instructed. I began to collect all the scraps of paper in and around the crate; I had been told to do that too."

Theon interrupted, "A rabbi sent a crate and robe to Eli? Please continue, Shamar, and we can discuss the rabbi later."

Shamar continued, "I began placing the scraps of paper into my pockets when three men came upon me, and before I knew it, two of them had grabbed me and began asking me questions as they were beating me. I tried to talk, but it was useless because each time I uttered a word, someone punched me. They were dressed like dock workers, and I never expected to be attacked in the docking area. I don't know who the men were or why they assaulted me, but I gave up on speaking. Shamar stopped for a moment, recalling the beating. "When the third man told the two men beating me to stop, they did and walked back to the man who was now holding the crate and giving orders. I was in pain and instinctively rolled up into a ball and began rocking myself in an effort to alleviate the pain. I grabbed a section of the robe in my other fist, and as I did, everything began spinning.

"The docks slowly disappeared from my vision, with darkness consuming me. I don't remember speaking to you, I don't remember how I got to your home, and I do not understand how all this took place. Please tell me, Theon, did your research disclose to you what happened to me and why?"

Theon thought for a few minutes, sipping his tea before attempting to answer Shamar. Parts of the puzzle were finally coming out: the crate, the robe, the rabbi, and perhaps even Eli. He was slow to answer Shamar because of what he had learned during his research and from the disappearing scroll. And now he needed to contemplate the involvement of a rabbi.

Theon began to think about the rabbi's part in this mystery and wondered whether this rabbi was the only person who knew about the crate and crystal. How did the rabbi know where the crystal was? How did he come by his knowledge? Did this rabbi understand the dangers associated with the crystal, and did he know of the evil beings who sought this crystal? Theon chose not to reveal too much to Shamar at the moment, but perhaps he would later.

"Shamar," began Theon, "I have only an impression as to why someone seeks the crystal that was hidden within your robe." Looking directly into Shamar's face, he added, "In addition, I am confident that together we can get the appropriate answers, especially to how you arrived here in Alexandria and conceivably how you might return to Colorado, wherever that is.

"I washed your robe last night. I must admit that I am very impressed with the quality craftsmanship used to assemble your robe. The crystals, the dragon, and especially the constellation Draco are exquisite.

"It is my conclusion, from facts I uncovered last night at the library, that you must accompany me to the library so that together we can assemble answers to both our curiosities and *why* fate has brought us together."

Theon continued, "We should employ a joint effort at putting together what each of us knows or can remember. Please understand that our lives are dependent on us learning the facts of this mystery as swiftly as possible because those seeking this information are ruthless individuals who use the assistance of assassins. Even I am uncertain of whom in Alexandria to trust; fortunately, from the information I read about you, I know you can be trusted. I am unclear but believe there is a way to get you back to your home. Please put on the robe, and we shall leave to the library together."

Shamar was baffled; how could Theon have read about him if he had just come back centuries in time? He thought briefly about Theon's request and was hesitant about putting on the robe again. What if he transported again to some other strange place and time?

When they finished eating, Shamar went to the kitchen and grabbed the robe. He saw the scraps of paper and gathered them up. Before returning to Theon, he looked at the designs on the robe that Theon had mentioned. He had not previously noticed the constellation Draco, the treasure chest, and the dragon, along with the numerous crystals and beads. This was indeed a special robe.

Walking back to the settee, Shamar began to remove Theon's nightgown. Theon noticed the deep purple bruises across Shamar's chest and abdomen. Shamar slipped out of Theon's nightgown and into the robe. Shamar again grasped the scraps of wadded newspaper and placed them into his pocket. The fit was incredible, as if the robe had been tailored for him. "I'm ready," Shamar stated.

Theon looked at Shamar with amazement and admiration. What he had read in the Jewish scrolls described Shamar perfectly. Shamar's unusual blond hair, blue eyes, and good physique fit the description flawlessly.

"Before we go, would you like me to help you in washing your face again? The cuts and bruises are healing, but perhaps a little attention is required. The facial bruising is not as bad as that on your abdomen."

Not waiting for an answer, Theon went to his well; he gathered some cloths and a small bowl of water. Returning to the settee, Theon attended to Shamar's wounds.

Taking a deep breath, Theon addressed Shamar. "It is time to go." Both exited Theon's front door and headed for the library. Mumbling to himself, Shamar was still hoping he had passed out and this was just a bad dream.

Arriving at the door to his office, Theon stepped in front of Shamar to unlock the door. To his surprise, when he began to place the key into the keyhole, the door was already slightly opened.

Theon turned to Shamar and whispered, "This door should have been locked. I have no idea who is inside." Cautiously Theon pushed the door open, slowly crossing the threshold while looking around into his office; he saw no one.

***

Quintus had waited all night nearby, just across the street from Theon's office, to keep watch. He had observed Theon at mid-afternoon as he returned home. Quintus now observed that the foreigner was with Theon as they walked through town and approached his office door. Quintus continued to watch them until both had entered the office together. Quintus was stunned at the foreigner's clothing. He had been unable to recognize it late last night, but in the sun's setting light, he believed he knew who this man must be.

Quintus recalled ancient literature about these unique robed individuals. *This foreigner is protecting Theon. I shall instruct my men to be watchful and respectful of this foreigner as he appears to be Theon's sentinel.*

***

Cautiously entering his office, Theon noticed a note on his desk. He picked it up and read it. "I have questions on your theory, father. Will you be available tonight to speak with me?" It was signed by his daughter, Hypatia.

Turning to face Shamar, Theon smiled and said, "My daughter was here today, and she left me a note questioning one of my most-recent theories. Perhaps Hypatia and I will get together soon to resolve her questions."

Theon looked to Shamar and said, "As soon as the classes are dismissed, I will take you to a secret room I found. I want to see your reaction." Theon walked to the street door and locked it.

Shamar was stunned. Theon's daughter was Hypatia; did he hear the name correctly? Was he actually interacting with the father of the world's first female mathematician? Theon began to speak, bringing Shamar out of his deep thought.

"Please take off your robe, as I need to sew something back under the emblem and talk to you about a few things before we go through the library."

Theon began to share with Shamar information he had learned from the scrolls, including a theory on how and why Shamar arrived in Alexandria. He also stated that he believed Shamar could possibly return home in much the same way he arrived. "This is why I believe fate has brought us together. I believe there may be information and perhaps items or individuals that are needed back in your time and that I am to help with retrieving the necessary items. Individuals who wear robes such as you are wearing have come and gone throughout time to assist or remove evil beings."

Slowly Shamar removed the robe. He asked Theon, "Theon did your research answer any questions about me? I understood what you just explained to me; however, is there anything else?"

Theon replied, "I don't know precisely, Shamar, but I can venture a guess that when you put on this robe and grasped the emblem, you were transported here. The crystal is said to contain many powers, and they remain unknown to me. Again, my conclusion is derived from information I have discovered in the secret room. I accept as fact that there is another hidden treasure room. That room may be your true quest. I will help you, as I want you to succeed. When you grasped the robe, the crystal apparently knew you were in trouble, and at that moment, it brought you here to Alexandria." Theon continued sewing on the robe while saying, "The men who roughed you up were looking for the crate; fortunately for you they did not realize the importance of the robe you were wearing. That leads me to think they were assassins. It was wise of the rabbi to send the robe and the crate separately. I believe the rabbi knew about this robe and was in search of the crystal, perhaps not realizing it was within his grasp. That is also a good sign as it tells us we are just one small step ahead of the seekers.

"The information that I have learned is staggering and dangerous. I also know that whatever is going on, it involved the great Aristotle. Aristotle knew of the treasures that Alexander the Great ordered hidden within this library, as he was one of the persons responsible for its inventory and safekeeping. He knew what was hidden and where. Likewise, I believe that after the death of Aristotle's nephew, which was ordered by Alexander the Great, Aristotle most likely was the person who moved the treasure in retribution for Alexander's actions against his relative.

"None of the close advisors or generals to Alexander was aware of the magnitude of information and treasures that Aristotle had concealed within the library.

"I was afraid to read or hold any scrolls that I found in the secret room because of what I learned previously from hidden scrolls here in the library, and I didn't yet know that I could trust you.
When I opened the first crate, I became dizzy and passed out. I don't know how long I was out, and I remained disoriented for a short time thereafter. That crate contained numerous scrolls. I was hesitant to touch or look at any scrolls in that crate because of what I experienced when opening and reading one of the scrolls."

Taking a deep breath, Theon continued, "The second crate sent a shockwave through my body. I have become aware, since that experience, that the chanting I heard earlier in the library was now comprehensible. There is much that I am uncertain of; however, I am convinced that I must help you to the best of my abilities."

Theon placed the robe back in Shamar's hand. "This Mr. Daniels has a lot of confidence in you, Shamar. I am of the opinion that if he knows anything about the robe and the crate, he would not send just anyone to retrieve such a package. I understood that he trusts you and knows that you would do exactly as he requested."

Deciding to go with the flow, Shamar smiled and gave a little chuckle. "Theon, I'm out of my element here. I'm a person who loves science and discovering new ways of doing things. I exercise and eat right, so I have the constitution for this. However, physics is my favorite subject. I chose to study anthropology only to be near Sophia Daniels, Eli's daughter.

"Sophia is the person you need here. Sophia is a linguist as well as an archeologist. She is brilliant, beautiful, and kindhearted. I cannot think of anyone who has an unkind word to say about her. I don't know what she sees in me. Sophia and her parents are brilliant.

"Or her father, who is curator of the museum, would also be useful here. When Sophia introduced her father to me, she immediately asked if he had a small position I might do at the museum. To my surprise, her father said yes. I appreciate her and enjoy her company. I miss her laughter, me trying to explain theories to her, and her explaining the past histories of different nations to me." Shamar was surprised at himself with the openness he was speaking to Theon with. He did not comprehend why he entrusted these feelings with Theon.

There was a silence that lasted for several moments before Theon spoke. Theon was glad Shamar was opening up to him. Perhaps, Theon felt, Shamar was recalling things, and that was good. "Are the Daniels Jewish?" asked Theon.

"Yes," answered Shamar.

Theon hesitated and then said, "I hear the last of the students leaving now. We will wait for a few moments, and then we will go."

Theon quietly unlocked his office door that opened into the library. Looking up and down the hall, he listened for any sounds. He heard nothing and whispered to Shamar, "I believe it is safe to go now. Follow me." They both walked quickly through the hall to the stairs.

Theon grabbed a torch from the wall and descended the stairs. He stopped when he reached the niche that held Alexander's statue. He pulled on the knees of the statue; they heard the stone-to-stone noise. Stepping up, Theon entered the small darkened opening and then turned, extending his hand to Shamar to help him step in. Looking around, Theon allowed a moment to let his eyes adjust to the darkness in the small foyer. Shamar watched as Theon walked to the wall and flipped the switch, closing off the door behind them.

As the door was closing, Shamar shivered and felt a slight uneasiness. Perhaps it was due to the darkness and the cool, confined area, but nevertheless, he questioned his decision to follow Theon.

Turning away from the switch plate, Theon motioned for Shamar to follow him. Theon began to walk swiftly into the tunnel toward the tunnel's light. Shamar remained just behind Theon, following as closely and silently as possible.

Reaching the cave opening, Theon stepped aside and gestured for Shamar to descend into the well-lit cave. Shamar was hesitant for a moment; however, stepping slightly in front of Theon, he slowly descended the steps into the cave. Shamar felt a pulsating energy softly touching his being.

Theon followed directly behind Shamar. Theon observed Shamar's reaction to the cave. Entering slowly, Shamar came into the larger area. He was amazed at his reflection on the ceiling and walls.

Moving slowly into the expanded room, Shamar stared at the candelabrum's lit blue candles yielding a glow throughout the room. Shamar saw the two crates as well as an empty pedestal where a third crate might have been. Everything was just as Theon had described.

"These crates are the same size as the crate I saw at the museum," Shamar stated.

Approaching the first crate, Shamar reached for the lid. Nothing happened to him; however, the candlelight from the candelabrum intensified as Shamar opened the crate. A gentle, incomprehensible whisper flowed through the room. Shamar seemed unaware of the delicate greeting; however, Theon understood the words and knew he had made the right decision about Shamar. The voice was welcoming Shamar to this holy place.

Shamar opened the lid and was instantaneously overcome by dizziness, followed by unsteadiness on his feet. Glancing into the crate, he began to spin faster, and blurry scrolls seemed to move before him.

Slowly Shamar began to grab scrolls and toss them out onto the floor. He turned around and saw Theon with opened arms moving toward him to steady him. "Thank you, Theon," said Shamar. Theon steered Shamar away from the crate to a corner where Shamar could sit and lean his back against the wall. "I don't know what came over me. I felt like I needed to take all the scrolls."

After looking them over for a few minutes, Shamar said to Theon, "I've been thinking that perhaps we need to put the like-symbol scrolls and color-coded scrolls together. Then we will decide which scroll to open first." Theon smiled back at Shamar and said he agreed.

Together they began to assemble the scrolls by categories. They began with the orange-sealed scrolls first since there were only two of them. The orange seal had a flaky wax seal. Shamar scraped the wax off the first scroll with little effort.

Theon assisted Shamar ever so gently in opening the scroll. Its text was in Hebrew, so Theon read it aloud. It began, "Years after the death of Alexander, a historian from the Library of Alexandria found scrolls sealed within a container. This container was rumored to have been used by Alexander during his conquest of Egypt.

"The container held three small scrolls written on parchment. Each yielded separate information that pertained to… (unreadable) these scrolls are now hidden within a secret room. (Unreadable)…scrolls signed in Thebes and documented items that Alexander showed the most interest in. The first scroll will have a dragon symbol upon it, which is said to represent the gathering of information necessary for… (unreadable). The second scroll will have stars formed in a particular constellation. Within the tail of this formation is a sentry shielding a pathway to the light, and the third scroll will have upon it the entrance to… (unreadable) containing information detailing where the necklace could be found."

Shamar and Theon looked at each other. Both were puzzled at what they had read.

"A necklace," said Theon. "On our way back to my office, we will stop by the Thebes bookcases and see what is there concerning jewelry." Shamar asked Theon which scroll he should open next. "I prefer sticking with the same color and completing that task before going to another color."

Together they gently scraped the old wax off the second scroll. Theon opened it; this scroll too was written in Hebrew, so Theon read it out loud. "As mentioned earlier, these crystals enable each of you to assemble at this gathering point. Remember that those using the special crystals and wearing the robe are always welcomed, as this room is a place of protection from evil."

Theon thought for a moment and then in an excited voice proclaimed to Shamar, "Each of you, each of you! There must be more than one individual with crystals and robes. Now I am positive that there is more than one person and the crystal underneath your robe is a traveling crystal, with possibly other abilities too. This must be the crystal they were referring to in the ornate ledger.

"Perhaps the other robe has a similar traveling crystal too. These gems are not just traveling crystals, Shamar, but communication gems as well, and perhaps more. We shall see; we need to find the answers here in these chests.

"Yes, Shamar, this answers why there could be more than one individual involved. Your robe contains many crystals protecting you from certain elements while allowing you to interact where needed. Shamar, we must leave now and seek information about this necklace. First let's place the scrolls together as you suggested, and when we come back, we will begin with what we think should be next. Our present priority is finding that necklace or information that will lead us to it."

Shamar gathered the scrolls, arranging them by color, symbol, or seal, and replaced them in the crate in an organized manner. Preparing to leave the secret room, Theon retrieved the parchment paper he had left earlier. Shamar and Theon began to move back to the main entrance of the cave, but Shamar stopped midway down the passage. Theon watched Shamar's reaction. Stepping closer to Shamar, Theon asked what he heard.

Shamar slowly and gently replied, "I am listening for an exact tone I was to anticipate."

They resumed their walk and exited back into the library. Shamar followed Theon, taking several turns, finally stopping at the bookcase of Thebes. Theon gathered scrolls on merchants who handcrafted jewelry with crystals. He gave them to Shamar and said, "Follow me."

Shamar and Theon walked down the library's hall heading back toward the staircase. Theon looked down the stairs, making sure the secret door had closed. He then placed the torch back into its holder. Shamar saw a scroll Theon might have dropped, and he picked it up off the floor.

Theon walked swiftly toward his office. He unlocked the door, and they entered. Theon locked the door behind them and gestured with his hand for Shamar to have a seat. Theon filled a pot with water and took it to the fireplace. He added more fuel to the fire to warm the pot of water for tea. Shamar watched Theon as he went about his business, and Shamar could not shake the sense that Theon was his guardian angel.

Shamar drifted into his own world, thinking about Sophia and her parents. He was concerned that they were in danger, and he wanted to rush home to tell all of them what had happened since they last spoke and most importantly to tell Sophia how much he cared for her. Shamar considered their situation. He wondered how the rabbi learned about the robe. Where did the rabbi get the robe? Did Eli understand the danger his family was in just because they were friends of the rabbi?

Together they began to read the Thebes scrolls as Theon translated them. They anticipated that their research would yield articles about the town's crystal jewelers and any written history connected with Alexander the Great. Theon found several articles of interest and shared them with Shamar for his opinion. Theon went to the fireplace and retrieved the teapot so they could drink hot tea while they discussed their task.

Their discussion, based on their new information, evolved into the conclusion that they belonged in Shamar's time and should return there as soon as possible. They believed that somewhere in the future, they could validate the information and continue the quest with the appropriate actions.

Shamar showed the odd scroll he had found in the hallway to Theon. Theon was surprised because this scroll had no title or place of origin upon it. Theon began carefully opening the fragile-looking scroll. Theon's voice lowered to soft whispers followed by long pauses as he deciphered the text.

Shamar realized something was dreadfully wrong. Theon's voice possessed a fearful tone. Theon stopped reading, slowly rolled the scroll closed, and looked to Shamar. Shamar could see that Theon's mind was spinning with a frightened anticipation from what he had read.

Softly, and still with a timid nervousness, Theon said to Shamar, "This scroll bears a warning about some very dangerous flasks. When those flasks are exposed to air, they will release a beacon throughout the universe to all who know of their power and purpose, including the evil ones. This beacon would be a signal that the jars have been found. Whoever wants them will try to take control of them. That beacon is the beginning of numerous chains of events. Those flasks are a Pandora's jar, and hopefully they have not yet been exposed to the air since what they can unleash into the world could be devastating. We must now make extraordinary efforts to close the beacon and keep the world from harm."

Theon stopped for a moment and continued, "We have both entered into this adventure lacking full knowledge of what and who we seek. The way is dangerous, and we must rely on each other for protection. The flasks are the gateway to those of dark character. An unknown outcome awaits us, and I believe we will encounter this dark foe and will need to fight for our survival."

Theon grasped Shamar's shoulders, and in a firm voice filled with determination said, "We must confide only in the people we know we can trust. That being said, our journey starts now. We must be prepared for the worst and expect the worst with this next step and each step thereafter. I suggest we go to the secret room and search for the scroll that contains the prayer alluded to in the scrolls we just read."

Pointing to the information on the scrolls, Theon stated, "We need more knowledge on how to use this crystal in connection with the crystals upon your robe, to understand their full purpose and potential to help us. Let's go back to the secret room."

Gathering the remaining scrolls, they swiftly headed for the secret room. They stopped back at the Thebes section only to return the scrolls from Thebes. Theon looked down the staircase and then decided not to take the torch.

He said, "We cannot take any chances, Shamar. We are escalating into a realm of unknown danger. The light within the cave will be sufficient."

Slowly and cautiously, both descended the stairs to the entrance of the secret passage. Theon pulled on the statue's knees. The door opened. Together they entered quickly into the dark area. Theon pushed the lever down, closing the statue's door. They watched as the statue's knee began to return to its appropriate position. Then Theon and Shamar rushed down the tunnel and into the cave.

Without hesitation, both approached the crate containing the scrolls. They rummaged through the crate, looking for the scroll with a particular symbol. After a moment, they found it. It was actually several small scrolls waxed together to appear as one. After examining the scrolls, both realized a few scrolls appeared to be missing.

They looked at each other, and Shamar said, "I am curious as to why a few are missing and who took the missing sections."

Theon thought for a moment and looked at Shamar. "We must hurry, Shamar, because someone is very close to finding what we need."

Breaking off one section of the scroll, Theon gently folded and placed the remaining scroll sections securely into his pouch, adding, "I deem this is the traveling scroll and that it will get us back to the museum in Colorado or wherever it wants us, so I will read the prayer but you must hold on to me, preferably very tightly.

"Shamar," said Theon in a stern voice, "I wish to caution you before we arrive at your homeland that we do not know who to trust. I have concerns about the rabbi, especially since he sent the crate and robe to Eli. I question whether Eli knew what the rabbi was doing. Was he working with the rabbi, or is Eli an unknowing pawn? I am extremely disturbed about the rabbi's actions, Shamar, extremely disturbed."

Shamar pondered this and then stopped. Shamar was contemplating whether Eli was likely to have anything to do with the cloak-and-dagger situation. "Theon," said Shamar, "I love Sophia, and I want to rescue her *and* her family. I suspect Eli knows nothing. I respect you and swear to you that I will be cautious of Eli." Taking Theon's hand into his, Shamar gave Theon a firm handshake while saying, "I want you to know that I will keep silent about this matter until you and I can discuss it and make a decision concerning Eli's trust."

The Thirteenth Stone of Aaron

Theon smiled at Shamar and thanked him for his trust. Shamar hoped they could return home in time to save Sophia and her family. Shamar grabbed Theon around the waist, firmly holding onto him, and said, "Let's travel." Both were confident that the small scrap from the scroll in conjunction with the robe would transport them back to Colorado.

Theon opened the small scroll and commenced reading the prayer aloud. Nothing happened. Theon began to reread the scroll, and again nothing happened. Theon looked to Shamar, and just as he was about speak, both felt a drawing sensation begin, accompanied by the light fading into darkness.

Shamar recognized the sign of what was transpiring; it was the same experience he had encountered when he was transported to Alexandria. Quickly Shamar pulled Theon's head closer to his chest for protection and warmth while at the same time placing his arm over the back of Theon's neck, allowing the sleeve to help keep Theon's neck sheltered from the bitter cold draft that was soon to come.

Then exceptionally cold current increased with the darkness, along with the awareness of an unrestrained spinning. Together they were passing through the darkness to what they hoped would be their desired destination.

CHAPTER FOUR
Patrick and Addison Examine the Contents of the Crate

P atrick sat at his desk, looking intently at the crate in the glass bookcase, pondering the new mysteries it presented. *Who crafted this crate, when, and why? Why does this crate remain veiled from history when, according to my father's journal, it is sought more than all other religious artifacts? When did my father learn about this crate and from whom?*

Patrick was especially troubled about the note to Eli from the rabbi, and in a state of bewilderment, he began to pace in the study. "Why would it warn not to touch the crate without wearing a robe?" Then a sudden realization struck him. "That moron Gabriel!" Patrick exclaimed as he recalled Gabriel's description of the man on the loading dock. "The man at the museum was not a monk; he was wearing the robe the rabbi sent to Eli!"

Addison arrived with Patrick's dinner tray. As he began to place the tray on Patrick's desk, Patrick moved toward Addison, touching his arm and saying, "Addison, I must speak to you. Please have a seat and hear me out."

Addison was taken off guard, noticing that Patrick had a softer appearance on his face and his voice was pleading for assistance.

Addison, wincing at this uncharacteristic gesture of familiarity, slowly and cautiously replied to Patrick, "Yes sir, I will listen to you."

Patrick began by moving the books from the chair to the floor, clearing off the seat so Addison could sit down. Returning to his chair, Patrick leaned forward and said, "I've been thinking about my present situation, and I've decided that a lot of things I've done since my father's death have not helped my circumstances.

"I want to begin by apologizing to you for my horrible behavior, not just this evening but for many years. I am sorry. Also I regret my behavior toward others too. For years I have alienated myself from those who might have been good friends to me. I thought that by following my father's notes, finding this crate would bring me fame and accolades from around the world. I expected to win respect and admiration.

"Sitting here at my desk and trying to understand my situation, I realize I am no different than my father. I have put this quest before all else. I remember how Mother and I missed him while he was gone, and when he returned home, he was too consumed with research to acknowledge us. Only occasionally did he realize we existed." Pausing for a moment to observe Addison's reaction, Patrick continued. "Is there any hope for me? Is there any chance I can make amends for my behavior? I don't want to be like my father, Addison. Please help me."

Addison studied the look on Patrick's face and could remember seeing that same look when he was up to something. For that reason, and recalling past requests for forgiveness without subsequent change, Addison was skeptical of Patrick's sincerity. He was also unsure of how to tell Patrick that not only had he burned bridges with others, but with some he had totally destroyed any likelihood of ever renewing a relationship.

Patrick could see Addison was at a loss for words, and he quickly interjected. "Have I screwed up so bad that there is no hope for me?"

"Yes and no, Patrick," Addison replied. "What I have observed over the years is just as you said, you have alienated many people with your arrogance and self-importance and yes, in some of the same manner as your father."

Addison continued, "Patrick, apologizing is only a very small step in correcting your past, and I don't think anyone will believe you. If you truly want to correct years of bad behavior, you must take socially acceptable steps to achieve your desired goal. However, it will take a lifetime of changing your actions, as well as your attitude toward everyone you deal with, and it can't be based on empty promises.

"People will not automatically forgive and forget your past actions, Patrick." Addison stopped for just a moment, trying to interpret Patrick's acceptance of

The Thirteenth Stone of Aaron

what he had said. Then he continued, "I am glad you have made this decision, Patrick, because your words tell me that you want to move forward and put the past behind you."

Addison scrutinized Patrick again. Patrick's eyes showed remorse, but his body language betrayed anger at what he was hearing. Patrick remained silent as he quietly stared at Addison. Addison sensed Patrick's irritation and realized he needed to be extra careful. Patrick's request for sympathy reeked of a ruse.

Patrick could tell from Addison's pause that he was indeed being careful. So Patrick replied, "Thank you. I'll work hard and not disappoint you or the memory of my parents. Also, I need your advice on a pressing issue facing me."

Addison needed a delay while he considered how to continue this conversation, so he stood up and said, "Please, let's go to the kitchen to talk and enjoy a fine meal together. My dinner is still on the stove waiting for me." Addison grabbed the dinner tray and led the way to the kitchen. Caught off guard by the abrupt move, Patrick meekly followed him into the kitchen.

When they arrived at the kitchen door, Addison opened it and said, "Please have a seat at my table. I'll prepare us some hot tea to go with our meal." In a few minutes, both were seated at the table enjoying dinner and tea together. Addison gave Patrick advice on how to correct his past with old friends.

Patrick brought up the subject of his father's crate by explaining to Addison his interpretation of the crate brought to him that evening. Patrick believed the crate to be the long-sought-after crate his father was searching for. He explained it was the correct size and shape and of the appropriate wood. Addison continued to listen as Patrick explained all his theories.

After they finished their dinner, Addison, with a little help from Patrick, straightened up in the kitchen, and both left for the study. Walking down the hall to the study, Addison remained suspicious of Patrick's change in attitude. His plan was to remain cautious in everything he said and did in Patrick's presence. Addison went directly to Patrick's chair, sat down, and began to sort thought Patrick's scraps of paper from the museum loading dock.

Addison was trying to determine several things about the scraps of paper. *One*, were the clippings were from the same newspaper or various newspapers? Were they the same month, day, and year or different? *Two*, what was the purpose of the scraps? Were they just added as filler, or did they have a purpose?

Addison tried to determine whether he could even tell what city the events in each article took place. Then Addison read the letter written to Eli from Rabbi Katz. Addison finished reading the letter and slowly placed the letter back down on the desktop. He looked over the top of his glasses at Patrick. Addison was trying to think of the correct words to let Patrick know what he thought of the scraps and the letter.

Patrick, being very anxious and impatient, interrupted Addison's moment of silence and asked, "Why would anyone need to wear a robe before they touched a crate?"

"Perhaps," began Addison, "it was because the crate and its contents were believed to be sacred, not cursed. The robe may be one of symbolism or respect to the contents within the crate, not fear. Indeed this resembles the actions of High Priest Aaron and how he dressed before entering sacred areas or using sacred items.

"If this crate held a curse, both you and Gabriel would probably have felt something immediately. So let's go with the religious or ceremonial theory rather than an attempt at protection. Do you know anything about the rabbi mentioned in the letter?"

Addison was especially watchful of Patrick's response because Addison had kept secret his knowledge of cooperation between Rabbi Katz and Patrick's father, Edward. Patrick replied, "No. But I intend to have my men investigate him for me."

Feeling very uneasy over this conversation, Addison decided this would be a good time to make excuses and leave. He felt a twinge of fear as he considered the possibility that Patrick might already know he was aware of the rabbi. Patrick watched him until he turned in the direction of his quarters and disappeared.

Arriving at his quarters, Addison very quietly closed the door behind him. After listening to make sure Patrick had not followed him, he walked to his closet and grasped a well-concealed leather journal off the top shelf. Slowly he walked to a chair and sat down. Looking at the journal's front cover, Addison recalled his reluctance to share with Edward his knowledge of Sago, an individual Mariah, Eli, and Edward despised.

Addison began to speak very softly into the emptiness of his room and said, "Edward, I was afraid of what your reaction might be if you knew I had personal knowledge of Sago. I tried my best to shield you and your family from Sago's obsession with that crate, the scrolls, and the special crystal Sago desperately wanted. I had been told of some of the despicable things he did to acquire the knowledge needed to find these treasures he was seeking.

"How could I tell you that Sago was my cousin without arousing your suspicion? I too detest the things my cousin has done and may continue to do in the future; I truly kept silent to protect you and your family. I worked hard to hide from Sago what you had found so Sago would leave you and your friends and family alone. I wanted Sago to think you came up empty-handed on your expedition and that the research was a failure. My hope was for Sago to leave all of you alone forever." Pausing for just a moment more, Addison arose, took a deep breath, and departed to return to the study.

Arriving back at the study with his journal in his hands, Addison could hear Patrick on the phone with someone. Addison's senses were charged with foreboding as he entered the study. He second-guessed his decision to share his journal's information with Patrick. Addison felt he must formulate a protection plan once he understood what Patrick was up to and who he had been secretly communicating with today.

Patrick was surprised when he noticed Addison had returned. Patrick saw the journal and was immediately interested in what was written within it. He wanted Addison to share it with him right away. Perhaps Addison's notes had the answers he was searching for.

Addison paused for only a moment and then took a seat at the desk. Patrick scooted his chair beside Addison's as Addison began to compare the notes from his journal to those in Edward's journal. After comparing the notes from Patrick's father's journal with Addison's notes, Addison became concerned. The two journals did not match at all. Why?

Addison muttered, "Something is not quite right, Patrick. Your father's entries are not consistent with what I remember, and your father's notes don't coincide with mine as they once did. Patrick, did you delete or change any of this information?"

"No," Patrick quickly replied.

Patrick immediately changed the subject by remarking that he believed the crate brought to the mansion had the potential of being the crate his father had spent so much of his time and money searching for.

Addison recognized that Patrick was anxious to hold and read his own personal journal, seeing Patrick's hands slowly creeping toward it. Addison slowly closed his journal and placed it at his side. He was still thinking about the discrepancies between the two journals and paid little attention to Patrick's remarks about the crate.

Addison was struck by the possibility that the revised notes in Edward's journal may have been a deliberate attempt to influence Patrick's search for the crate. The information in it was incorrect and barely legible. He was also concerned that Patrick showed no curiosity regarding the fact that his father's journal had been altered.

Addison returned his attention to Patrick, realizing that he was continuing on about the crate. He was outlining a plan for their examination of the crate and speculating about how they might start their investigative process. Grabbing his journal, Addison walked over to the fireplace and placed his journal on a small coffee table.

Returning to the desk, Addison said out loud, "Patrick, it is always best when working with archaeological items to have numerous soft cloths and a good dry paintbrush readily available." Opening the desk drawer, Addison swiftly grasped and placed cloths on the top of the desk and then a second pile of cloths near him. Atop each pile of rags, Addison placed a small dry paintbrush.

Patrick went to the glass bookcase and retrieved the crate. Addison remarked to Patrick the need to return his journal back to his room. Patrick appeared to be in a trance but nodded in agreement with Addison. Slowly walking back to his desk, Patrick gently set the crate down. Next Patrick placed his father's journal back into the desk drawer, closed the drawer, and locked it. He anxiously awaited Addison's return.

Addison returned again and noticed a look of excitement upon Patrick's face. Addison went to the desk to begin the examination of the crate with Patrick. Both studied the crate for several minutes. Addison thought of all the years Edward had searched for this crate and now, with altered information in Edward's journal, Patrick had found the crate! *How curious, that he was able to accomplish this*, Addison thought to himself.

Together Addison and Patrick began to examine the outside of the crate. Paying attention to every detail, they noted that the crate was a true work of art. Its smooth outer surface had been made from acacia wood, a characteristic that Edward had said was a must. Advancing their search, Patrick and Addison checked for traps and markings. Finding none, Patrick eagerly opened the lid.

What they saw were three beautiful and flawless crystal flasks. Each flask was crowned by a different-colored stopper that had a distinctive illustration upon it. The stoppers appeared set just within the flask openings, adding a timeless radiance to each crystal masterpiece.

Both took in deep breaths of astonishment. Addison thought he glimpsed fine, almost invisible vapors softly flowing and quietly dispersing upward from the flasks. Each flask's vapor matched the colors of its stopper. In his eagerness to delve further into the crate, Patrick was oblivious to the vapor's presence.

Realizing that Patrick wanted to lead the investigation, Addison took a position at the desk, where he prepared to take notes as each flask was removed from the crate to the desktop. With extreme care, Patrick gingerly wrapped his hands around the first flask. Gently removing it from the crate, he slowly placed it upon a soft cloth on the desktop.

"This crystal flask is amazingly light," Patrick remarked to Addison.

Addison thought for a moment that perhaps the vapors lightened the flask's weight. Patrick and Addison could see that the main body was decorated with red etchings that twinkled as though the flask had just been created. The two awestruck men were looking upon the figure of a snake's delicate body with red and golden hues glistening upon the adorning stopper. Addison opened the curtains so they could examine the flasks in the daylight.

Addison returned to the desk and began to take notes. He remarked out loud to Patrick, "The craftsmanship is of the highest quality, and I am certain the highlighted crystal art we are observing is from a bygone era. This appears to be an object d'art of the magnificent crystal workers from Thebes. They are credited as the creators of crystalline art. Indeed a lost art that not only requires that the paint be sealed in camphor for a long period of time, but also that the artist be very skillful in selection of the tools required to ensure the image lives on indefinitely.

"Today's craftsmen cannot hold a candle to the talent of these individuals who lived hundreds of years ago. The mixture of elements they used for creating their paint has never been duplicated."

Patrick, still astonished at the beauty of the crystals, said to Addison, "Look at how the delicate sketch of a snake is magnificently etched between these glass walls. And this elegantly stained etching appearing between the outer and inner sections of glass skillfully emulates reality by emphasizing the depth, yielding a lifelike artistic character to the colored sand within the flask.

"Moreover, the way the snake's golden eyes are highlighted gives the impression that the snake is looking at us. "Perhaps," Patrick added slowly, "it actually is watching us."

He slowly turned the flask in a circular motion, surveying the entire etching and giving particular attention to the areas with color, which were illuminated by the light from within the room and emphasized the crystal's beauty. Then he felt dazed, as it seemed like the image actually touched his eyes in a soft and subtle way.

Addison was surprised by Patrick's reaction as he awkwardly put the crystal down on a cloth and began staggering backward away from the flask, trying to find his chair.

"Are you OK?" Addison asked, concern reflected in his slightly raised voice.

Patrick did not answer. He looked terrified. Addison rushed to his side. Grabbing a cloth, Addison pitched it over the crystal flask while still watching Patrick. He was concerned because Patrick appeared to be in a trance. Gently, and with small strides, he guided Patrick to his chair and helped him sit down.

Realizing that this had taken him by surprise, and still in a daze, Patrick looked at Addison, and then back at the covered crystal. "Addison," Patrick began, his voice rich with emotion, "I had a vision that I was in a room and someone was whispering my name." Placing the palms of his hands over his eyes, Patrick continued, "There is a sensation around my eyes; it feels like a hot swelling, and my vision is foggy. I don't remember anything else, just a room, and my name was whispered. And there is numbness around my eyes."

He continued in a shallow voice, "What could this be, Addison? What could this be?" Fumbling for a cloth, Patrick grasped one and began wiping sweat from his forehead. Then, in spite of his clouded vision, Patrick covered the flask with a larger cloth, and in an unconcerned manner, he dropped the covered flask back into the crate.

He then covered the flask with another cloth, his emotions revealing a fear of the flask and concern that the snake might still be watching him. Confused, Patrick hastily scribbled semi coherent notes into his ledger with a description of the vision and his feeling of fear. Addison noticed that the script Patrick had just entered resembled the handwriting in Edward's journal. Addison and Patrick waited before examining another flask.

Standing again at the side of his desk, Patrick retrieved the next crystal flask. Patrick placed it upon a soft cloth. Addison remarked that if they needed to finish this later, they could. Ignoring his comment, Patrick gathered extra cloths, ensuring that he and Addison would be better prepared.

Again Patrick beheld a beautiful cylindrical crystal flask with an etching between the glass walls that was mostly concentrated in a particular area with delicate, precisely colored designs. The artwork he held in his hands was reminiscent of the most vivid starry night sky he had ever seen. A stopper suspended just within the opening was adorned with a dragon's head, regally shaded with various blue hues.

Its colored sands were soft blue gray with contrasting pale silver and white areas that looked like a group of stars forming a pattern. After a closer look, he saw the stars appeared to be brilliant silver. Patrick asked Addison what he thought. "Oh my, Patrick," Addison replied. "I do believe this is the constellation Draco. How magnificently it has been portrayed."

As with the other flask, Patrick started to turn the flask in a circular motion, this time at a much slower rate. Again Patrick felt wonder and dread shoot through him. He slumped back into his chair and stared for a long time at the flask. Addison dropped his pen, went to Patrick's side, and asked, "What happened this time?"

Patrick gazed back at Addison, finding it difficult to speak and wondering how much he should tell him. Taking hold of Addison's hand and looking into his eyes, Patrick, in a soft but noticeably muddled voice, replied, "I was somewhere else and felt like something really bad was about to happen. It was like I was really there. There was a jolt of energy through my mind and body. And then everything that was taking place around me was terrible. I could see it. I could feel it. And I couldn't stop horrible things from happening to me."

Terrified, Patrick questioned whether they should continue. Addison returned to his notes and recording not only all Patrick had said but also his changes in demeanor.

Addison speculated that perhaps a special robe was necessary to view these flasks. After reflecting on the recent events, he supplemented his notes. "Patrick's description is most curious; a jolt of energy through his mind and body, a foreboding, and then witnessing an event yet to happen that filled him with terror." Briefly, Addison's mind traveled back to Patrick's father and the items Edward had hidden. Addison was curious now that perhaps Edward had known more than he had told him concerning the footlocker and its contents that had been brought back from the Alexandria dig.

Looking into the crate, Addison cautiously draped a cloth over the dragon flask and then gently placed it back in the crate. Addison decided it would be wise to suspend any further examination of flasks until he could finish his notes. If something else were to take place, he might forget important details. However, shortly, he began to experience the sensation that he had to examine the last flask. As he stared at the crate, this feeling grew into an obsession.

After a long, thoughtful pause, Addison removed the last flask from the crate. He observed the usual glass stopper that was suspended just inside the flask. This decorative stopper was adorned by a figure of a partially opened scroll. Having no ill feeling from this flask, Addison cautiously set it gently on a soft cloth on the desk.

Patrick, sitting up in his chair, directed his eyes toward this flask and its decorative stopper. He scrutinized its defining features: the stopper boasted a finely etched scroll that hovered just above the opening. The etching on the flask defined an open scroll displaying an inscription that exhibited faint wording between the walls of the crystal's glass. Gold flakes seemed to be intertwined among the words, which were etched in black.

The sand within was a very light brown, almost white in color; it twinkled with iridescent white, silver, and gold hues. The colored etchings glittered with a golden twinkle and a silvery gray hue.

Patrick opened one of the desk drawers and grabbed some magnifying glasses. Speaking to Addison, he said, "Perhaps these will help." Patrick offered a magnifying glass to Addison, who pulled the flask closer.

The Thirteenth Stone of Aaron

Leaning in toward the flask, Addison was preparing to jot down its pictorial or word representations. To his astonishment, each of the small etchings was a miniature scroll etched with a distinctive mark. *Oh my,* Addison thought, *there is a sword woven completely down the side of these scrolls. Its shape is visible because of the words used to make it a picturesque sword. The calligraphy is elegant.* Addison chose to look deeper to decipher the lettering, identify the type of sword inscribed, and make note of the mysteries unfolding from this flask.

Addison felt a sensation starting at his fingertips and running up his hand, continuing through his arm, and climaxing in what felt like starburst throughout his entire body. Uncertain of possible consequences from just touching the flask, he reached for a cloth. A soft whisper engulfed both his ears, blocking all other sounds. A feeling of tender affection pulsed through his heart, and he no long felt a sense of danger; rather he felt that whoever was addressing him was providing him with a gentle, motherly warning about Patrick. The soft voice urged him to be cautious of the evil residing within Patrick's body.

The warning ended with hushed whispers of potential danger from an unspeakable source. Addison vividly recalled Edward's mention just before leaving Alexandria of a soft whisper that warned him of danger. Edward had quoted to Addison the words of the warning: "A dark, twisted foe has reopened the door to a long and difficult journey that will have sad endings for some and fulfillment for others."

Addison considered what each flask had revealed and the verbal words and accompanying sensation he was not prepared for. Addison's lips were moving as he produced an inaudible whisper, telling himself, "This treasure was not what I had anticipated. It is more, much more than I could ever have imagined. Edward hid secret items he brought back with him from the Alexandria dig. Perhaps Edward knew of these flasks, their purposes, and their affiliation with the robe."

Addison recalled each flask's excellent craftsmanship and the fine, artistically placed sand. Just the effort to forge these flasks required incredibly detailed talent. Addison's thoughts delved deeper into the issue. *What do these three flasks represent? Who were the craftsmen, and why were they made? How did Patrick learn of these flasks, and how did he acquire them?*

Addison spoke his concerns clearly to Patrick. "I'm curious, Patrick. Someone altered the information you have been following, and much of it is wrong; I don't understand how you found these precious flasks."

Patrick looked to Addison, considered what he had said, and ignored the question. Patrick remarked, "We definitely need the help of Sophia and her parents. We have to reopen communication with them, and I must do whatever it takes to get this project moving forward.

"I know I can't succeed without Sophia's knowledge and support. I also need the help of her parents. I have been such a fool to think I could step in and pick up the quest without the necessary expertise of archaeologists and linguists. Oh, Addison, I allowed my ego to govern my thoughts of fame and fortune, and in doing so, I lost a friendship that I still long for. I have wanted to be a part of Sophia's life for some time."

Turning to gaze into the fireplace, Patrick remarked out loud to Addison, "Why couldn't I visualize what was in third flask? Why was it foggy to me? Was it because the snake skewed my vision? What were you able to see in the third flask?"

Hearing nothing, Patrick continued, "What my father worked so to achieve has me frustrated and puzzled. I don't understand why or how he chose to investigate. Seeing these flasks and having the disturbing feelings and visions from them leaves me even more puzzled."

Addison finally spoke. "These flasks have imbued you and me with feelings, visions, and warnings, and I agree with you that we desperately need help. However, the way you pushed people away from you, and the manner in which you drove them away, getting people to help us may be difficult or impossible.

"Your father and Eli were friends, and remember, Mariah also helped your father. I agree with you that you do need their help. However, before you can recover their trust, you must be honest with everyone, especially yourself."

Tired of discussing his shortcomings, Patrick changed the subject and snapped back, "Addison, I want to investigate everyone who worked with my father. Would you happen to have any names in your notes?"

Before Addison could turn to face Patrick, Patrick had spun around and was facing Addison. It appeared that Patrick had anticipated Addison's next move both physically and verbally. The appearance on Patrick's face changed to that of a predator. "Additionally, Addison," demanded Patrick arrogantly, "I need to understand why this crate and a robe were sent to Eli and not to me. It was my father who was head of this research to find the crate, and I believe this was my father's objective and not Eli's."

Addison was stunned. *So that's how he found the crate. He stole it from Eli. Is that why there is no robe as described in the rabbi's note?*

Addison stood up, wanting to go back to his quarters. Patrick's choice of words about his opinion that the crate now belonged to him caused him concern. He understood that Patrick's determination to find the crate and the effort he had recently invested had led to this impression. It was obvious Patrick would never consider that the crate might belong to anyone else.

Ultimately Patrick calmed down. In a softer tone, he said, "Addison, I don't know where I can hide this crate. The visions scare me, and I would like to hide myself and this crate from the world. I realize you may be the only person who can help me, both in doing something with the crate and advising me concerning appropriate behavior."

Addison thought for several minutes before responding. Finally he said, "I believe it is proper for you to apologize to Eli for what happened at the docks. Be honest to Eli about involving others in helping you to steal the crate. I also have experienced a sensation from the crystal flasks that cause me significant concern.

"Remember, it will take time for people not only to accept your apology but also to realize it is genuine. Be patient, as this is your first step on the path we discussed earlier. It is a long and difficult path, but you can be successful if you keep your thoughts and intentions focused on meaning what you say and saying what you mean. Now go and apologize. I will be here when you return."

CHAPTER FIVE
Eli Learns of Rabbi Katz Death.

Colorado

Eli was getting impatient. *What happened to Shamar?* He left his office and strolled into the reception area, walking up to Karrie's desk. She bid Eli a good morning and extended her hand, offering the mail. "These arrived overnight; and you have two appointments today, one at eleven a.m. and a second at two p.m."

"Thank you, Karrie," Eli said as he accepted the mail. "Has Shamar contacted you yet?"

"Yes," she replied. "He said he would meet you in just a bit. He has possession of both the boxes and said he was busy gathering a lot of scraps of paper. Would you like me to give him a call and get an update?"

Eli thought for a moment and responded, "Perhaps he doesn't want to be seen in a robe and is changing back into his street clothes." Eli had just finished with his statement when a special delivery carrier arrived with packages for him. Eli took the small package and envelope, letting Karrie sign the receipt.

"If you hear from Shamar, let me know immediately," Eli said, returning to his office. Placing the mail on his desk, Eli sat down and studied the envelope. The return address was from an attorney he was unfamiliar with. He placed the small package aside and opened the large envelope.

Eli dumped the contents from the envelope onto his desk. Two items plopped out. Eli looked to see if anything else remained; there was nothing.

Eli recognized the handwriting and the wax seal of Rabbi Katz on the small envelope. The other piece of paper was an unfolded letter. The letterhead matched the return address of the large envelope. It was from a New York attorney. Eli was concerned at receiving information from an attorney he didn't know.

Eli opened the rabbi's letter first. To his surprise, two keys clattered onto his desk. One key had a tag attached with finely written instructions, and the other key looked very old and fragile. Choosing to read the note on the tag first, Eli grabbed his glasses from his jacket pocket. He twisted the tag toward him and began to read the instructions. Surprised at what he had read, Eli sat down at his desk, contemplating the consequences of this small note.

While mentally processing the contents of the note, he cautiously removed the tag and placed the instructions in his slacks pocket. Holding both keys in the palm of his hand, Eli stared at them, bewildered. Placing both keys in his other pocket, Eli continued to examine the information sent to him. Although confused about the keys and their mysterious instructions, Eli decided to follow the instructions. Holding the small envelope in his hand, Eli noticed what appeared to be strange marking on the inside of the envelope.

Grasping the envelope, Eli noticed writing on the inside of the envelope was faint and barely legible. Gently disassembling the envelope, Eli discovered a secret note from the rabbi. Eli began to read the note.

> I found an archaeological item that is invaluable and sought after by many who wish to use it for its perceived abilities. One particular individual is very evil and thinks it will help him rule the world.
>
> I realized too late that someone understood what I had found and was watching my every move. I know this someone will eventually kill me

to take possession of the artifact. I apologize that your family is now in grave danger because of our friendship and correspondence. After sending the items to you, I was aware of how close this evil individual was in his knowledge of me and my comings and goings. I am so sorry that I placed your family and myself in this lethal position. This evil person will hunt for you and your family because they have knowledge that I communicated with you and they will believe you know as much as I do about the artifact, robe, and crate.

Confide in no one your knowledge of what we have talked about and especially what I have sent you. Please use the key at the address enclosed below, and tell no one of this cabin, as it is your family's refuge from individuals who will murder all of you, not only to gain possession of the items I sent you but to guarantee you never speak to anyone. Please, reexamine everything I have sent. Look at all my correspondence with new eyes to find and study my clues. My hope is that you find the necessary answers and directions to defeat the evil.

I have left you clues as to where I hid the treasure within my correspondence. The crate and robe I sent you are items they seek, which is why I sent them separately. I must get this to you as soon as possible as I am certain I do not have much longer to live.

Sitting back in his chair for a few minutes, Eli pondered the message. After thinking for a while, he gently folded the envelope back into its envelope shape and placed it into his pants pocket. He would search later to find the clues that would clarify this mystery.

Eli slowly opened the letter from the attorney and began to read it:

Dear Dr. Eli Daniels,

I am Roberto Miranda Esq., the administrator for Rabbi Benjamin Katz. I write to inform you that Rabbi Katz has passed and you are mentioned in his last will and testament.

It is hard to believe he will no longer be with us, and we will all miss him. Mr. Katz has been a client of mine for several years, and he spoke highly of you on many occasions. During his most recent conversation with me, he requested that I guarantee that you are given two items without delay upon his passing. Those two items, a robe and a crate, have been mentioned to me verbally and are included in his will. I will be going to the rabbi's home tonight, and when I find the items he spoke of, I will overnight them to you at your museum address, per his instructions.

Should you have any questions, please do not hesitate to contact me at the phone number on my letterhead and business card.

Respectfully,
Roberto Miranda Esq.

Eli was stunned; he found it hard to believe that the rabbi was dead. Slumping back in his chair, he began to recall recent conversations and ask himself questions. Eli was puzzled because just a few days earlier the rabbi had called to inform him that he was sending him two boxes, and he had looked forward to spending time with him and his family. He sounded so upbeat and happy. *What happened? How did he die? Did he have an accident or sudden illness? And most of all, what are these dire warnings about?*

Slowly, Eli walked to his office door, opened it, and walked to Karrie's desk. Eli told Karrie, "Please cancel all of my appointment for the next few weeks, and when you are done, you may take that time off with pay. Thank you."

Karrie was astonished by what she heard, and with a puzzled voice replied, "Yes sir, I'll do that right away. Is there anything else I can help you with?"

Eli slowly turned and walked back to his office. She could tell from his demeanor that he was not approachable. Karrie watched as Eli slowly returned to his office and closed his office door. She heard the click as he locked it. Karrie promptly began to comply with Eli's request.

The Thirteenth Stone of Aaron

Eli walked over to the file cabinet and removed his black book and a plastic accordion filing folder. He tossed both of them onto his desk. Then he walked to the safe and opened it. He removed a shoebox and carried it to his desk.

Sitting down, he removed the lid from the shoe box, grabbed its contents and placed the pile of letters face up on his desk. He began sorting the letters by month and year according to the postmarks. Eli placed the latest correspondence at the bottom of the pile.

Staring at the small package, Eli paused, wondering whether he should open it or continue with the process of shutting down his office. Time passed as Eli continued to stare at the small package. He realized he was not thinking rationally. Recalling his last conversation with the rabbi, he was now fearful. *Why did the rabbi send me the robe and crate, and why must the robe be worn in conjunction with the crate? What am I missing? Could his warning be legitimate? Has my family been placed in harm's way and why?* Eli became panicky at what might happen to him and his family.

Dear Eli,

I am happy you will soon be in possession of the robe and crate. I hope to meet with you shortly to give you my verbal explanation of these items, which have a long history. My pursuit has ended! Be aware that before you open or touch the crate, you *must* be wearing the robe. You are the person I chose because you are trustworthy and because my prayers and meditation brought me to the conclusion that you must be the one. Over the years we have had an honest relationship where we can communicate without judgment.

Please allow me this indulgence in asking you for such an imposing favor. These items must never be considered for public view, and the robe must be worn only during activity with the crate and its contents. I also enclosed a key and directions for you.

Respectfully,
Rabbi Katz

Eli's memory jolted him as he recalled that Shamar was doing an errand for him that involved retrieving the crate and the robe. Eli rushed from his office in an attempt to get to the docks and check on Shamar. Taking only a few steps into the outer office, he remembered the need to lock his office door. Grabbing the keys from his pocket, he quickly returned to the office door and locked it. Turning in a hurried manner and then sprinting toward the elevator, he noticed his daughter approaching him.

Sophia saw her father and called out, "Hello, Father." Hearing her voice, Eli stopped and extended his open arms to Sophia. Eli was thinking to himself, *She is moving so slowly, and I need to hurry to the docks.*

Sophia was her usual happy self, and she seemed eager to greet her father; Eli anticipated that she might have news of Shamar, but she was preoccupied with the magazines she was holding. Taking Sophia into his arms, Eli gave her a hug and then a gentle kiss on the forehead.

"Hello, Sophia, how is your morning?" he said.

"Great," Sophia replied. "I am anxious to help Shamar on the new Egyptian exhibit. I found these old magazines, and I think they might help with ideas for the display you assigned him to work on."

Eli took the magazines from his daughter and placed them on his secretary's desk. Then he guided Sophia toward the elevators. "Sophia, have you heard from Shamar today?" he asked.

"No. Not yet. Have you heard from him, Father?"

Eli was concerned. "Actually, I'm on my way to the loading dock to meet him."

Stepping into the elevator with Sophia, Eli pressed the button. He was staring down at his feet, trying to hide the uneasiness welling up within him. Eli, recalling particular words from the rabbi's letters, became anxious about the crate and robe.

He regretted not giving extra attention to what, at the time, he had interpreted as ramblings from an elderly gentleman. Nevertheless, the rabbi's correspondence had recently been more frequent than usual, and his most recent letter was very much out of the ordinary.

Am I allowing my imagination to put too much into his writings? Do I need to protect my family from the things the rabbi predicted? What if the rabbi's death was not natural?

The Thirteenth Stone of Aaron

I don't understand why he chose me to share his secrets with; however, I realize his choices were not idle.

Have I placed my family and Shamar's lives in danger? Why did he send me a robe and crate? What significance do they have with what he has spoken and written to me about? I need to complete the organization of his correspondence and try to decipher what he was warning me about.

"Is there something wrong, Father?" Sophia asked, noticing his unusual mood.

Eli looked up at Sophia and answered, "I hope not. I sent Shamar to the loading docks earlier this morning to see if my two boxes had come in, and Shamar has not gotten back with me."

"That does not sound like Shamar!" Sophia exclaimed. Eli agreed.

Arriving at the dock, Eli and Sophia began to look for Shamar. They saw no one. The dock was empty of people and somewhat dark; its only light was from the large skylights above. Eli asked Sophia to wait for him in a hushed voice.

Cautiously, Eli walked around and examined each loading dock, its entire loading area, as well as the surrounding area. He checked the shelves as he passed them, looking up and down the aisles. He spotted the red box on the floor. It had been opened and thrown upon the ground. Eli moved toward the box. He found Shamar's clothing in the lid of the red box. *So Shamar must be wearing the robe,* Eli thought to himself.

Eli gathered a few wadded-up newspaper scraps from the dock's floor and stuffed them into his pocket. He quickly scanned the scraps, observing the newspaper's name and date in the upper section. It was published by a New York printer.

An obituary was neatly folded and lying on the floor. Lettering of this individual's memorial was highlighted. Eli scanned the highlighted section, which read, "I recall an experience in which I had received similar communications. Those memories haunt me due to my underestimating the opposition. Unless swifter actions are taken, the same foe who escaped his bonds eons ago will unleash everything he can upon humanity. This foe has been silent for too many years and has undoubtedly increased his abilities." *How odd,* he thought after reading the paper.

Pulling the red box closer to him, he confirmed that the robe was missing, and only Shamar's clothing was available. Also missing was the crate. Placing more scraps into his pocket, he turned to face Sophia and said in a loud voice, "Sophia, I need you to go over to the west wall and turn on the lights please."

Sophia didn't hesitate; she rushed to the panel and flipped the switch, turning the lights on. Eli continued to examine the area where the paper had been thrown about. Bending down he saw some blood on the ground and a few bloody scraps of paper, along with Shamar's cell phone. He picked up the scraps. Glancing around, Eli spotted Shamar's backpack upon the dock floor. Eli became panicky about Shamar's safety. It was obvious something was wrong.

He couldn't believe this. Shamar and the crate were missing without a sign, except for a little blood, and the person who sent the crate had warned him about murderers and was now dead. He shivered with fear and was beginning to feel sick. His family had to be protected, and he wondered if he was too late to protect Shamar.

He heard the unmistakable noise of the overhead light switch being thrust upward, and immediately following this sound, the lights illuminated the docks. Eli could hear Sophia running toward him at a fast pace. He didn't want her to see the blood, so he used the red box to cover the stained floor. He grabbed Shamar's backpack and cell phone and quickly stuffed Shamar's clothing and cell phone into Shamar's backpack, noticing that the phone was off...

"We need to call Shamar as soon as possible. Do you have his number?" Eli said to Sophia.

"Yes," she replied, adding, "What's wrong?"

Forcefully grabbing Sophia's arm; he turned her around in the direction of the door. "Good, Sophia. Let's return to my office immediately."

An unfamiliar nervousness crawled up his spine as he placed the strap from Shamar's backpack over his shoulder. Walking at a fast pace to the door, Eli pushed the dock entrance door open; his pressing thought was to exit the docks as quickly as possible, to protect Sophia from any danger that might be lurking nearby. He couldn't shake an impression that he was being watched. His mind, overloaded with fear and anticipation of the unknown, was recalling things that the rabbi had shared with him verbally and in writing.

Eli tucked Sophia's arm under his and briskly continued toward the elevators. Sophia was at a loss for words, as she had never seen her father act in this manner. Her father called her by her full name and not the usual nickname. Also, he was silent and distant; she sensed the alarm that was present in his demeanor. Sophia was becoming distressed. They both heard the dock door slam behind them, and Sophia felt her father recoil at its sound.

Neither Sophia nor Eli observed the figure hidden just around the corner at the docks. Nevertheless the individual concealed in the shadows had listened and took notice of not only both of them but also their actions and conversation.

The watcher observed that Eli had picked up scraps from the dock floor and placed them in his pocket. This individual also observed Eli studying the red box and grabbing the backpack. Notation was given about their conversation concerning a man named Shamar.

This phantom felt Eli's fear as it permeated through the docks with each clue Eli uncovered. Eli's fear was feeding the phantom's excitement, and he desired more. The phantom knew it was just a matter of time until this victim, Eli, would meet him face-to-face, and at this meeting he would then be able to absorb and delight in consuming of all of Eli's fear before extinguishing his life.

***

Within minutes they arrived at Eli's office. Eli opened his office door, allowing Sophia to enter first; following Sophia, Eli shut the office door behind them.

Sophia quickly called both of Shamar's phones, but there was no response, just an answering machine. With tears in her eyes, Sophia looked at her father and stated in a questioning voice, "Where could Shamar be? Is he all right? What is going on, Father?"

Eli stared at Sophia for a moment because he didn't know the answer and he was afraid of learning what had taken place on the docks. Eli understood Sophia cared a great deal for Shamar. This added feelings of remorse to his present situation.

Eli took in a deep breath and said, "We are going to go home. I have something I need to discuss with you and your mother."

Sophia walked directly up to her father and asked in a firmer tone, "What's the matter with you, Father? What are you trying to hide from me, and what have you gotten Shamar into?"

Eli was startled by Sophia's reaction but chose not to answer her; instead he went to the phone and called Mariah. He spoke briefly to his wife, asking her to cancel all appointments for the next few weeks. He said he needed to discuss something with her and Sophia and that the discussion was of the utmost importance. Walking to the safe, Eli removed several large envelopes. Sophia asked her father again, "Father, what is going on? Is Shamar OK, or is he in trouble?"

Eli could not look at Sophia to answer her question. He was conscious that a threat to his family existed. He did not know what he should do, who he could trust, or exactly how he was going to protect his family. Again the rabbi's words of caution crept through his mind, warning him of danger.

Placing the envelopes, along with all other correspondence, on his desk into Shamar's backpack, Eli looked at Sophia and said, "We need to go home now. I will answer all your questions in the privacy of our home. I believe our lives are in danger, and I hope Shamar is all right."

Grabbing the backpack with one hand and Sophia's arm with his other, he directed her from his office. Neither said anything as they headed at a fast pace toward the parking garage.

Arriving at his parking space and clinging tightly to Sophia, Eli opened the door and pushed Sophia into the passenger's seat. Rushing to the driver's side, he opened his door and threw the backpack onto the rear seat. Starting the engine, he began to exit the museum's garage.

On his way out, he stopped to speak to the attendant. "Sophia will be back later to get her car. Make sure it is not towed."

Eli rolled his window back up without listening to the attendant's reply. Eli said out loud, "Please be quiet, Sophia, as I must think. You can listen to music if you want, but I need to consider all my options to make the appropriate decision."

"Father, what is wrong?" Sophia said in a determined voice. Eli's expression told her to be silent.

Eli mulled over what he could remember of the rabbi's words, especially those that were presented with an intentional inflection in his voice. The rabbi had provided hints or warnings that Eli needed to use caution with everyone he encountered but no explanation as to why. Eli's first thoughts went back to their initial meeting in which the rabbi had given reference to Abraham. Eli could not remember clearly but thought it had to do with something that was passed down and given to King Solomon. Eli still didn't understand the connection between these statements and potential danger. However, that verbiage was a theme the rabbi repeated frequently to Eli.

Eli thought about how caught up in the rabbi's history lesson he had become, acknowledging that he had failed to understand that the rabbi was cleverly passing information to him in the form of a biblical lesson. *I do remember that at our second or third meeting, he became impatient with me and slapped his hand on my desk to get my attention. It was at that moment that I believed this was the rambling of an elderly man who just needed someone to listen to him.*

What a mistake! I misunderstood the message he was attempting to give me. I regret not asking more questions, He had the ability to put in plain words events, people, and a particular timeline so well that I could envision the happenings as if I was there. He was definitely steeped in the biblical history he shared with me.

Hopefully in his correspondence I can find the references I need. I don't understand the importance of the robe or crate. Why were they so important to the rabbi? What could be worth killing for? He never mentioned what might be in the crate.

During their ride home, Sophia was aware of her father's emotional state; she had never witnessed him like this before. It was not the silence that concerned her but his facial expression, the manner in which he was conducting himself, and especially his driving. He wove in and out of traffic with aggressive movements that occasionally betrayed anxiety. He gunned the car at yellow lights and rolled through stop signs. This was highly abnormal behavior, and it frightened her.

Sophia was trying to understand why or how Shamar was involved. Adjusting her safety belt, Sophia closed her eyes and said a silent prayer for her family and Shamar.

CHAPTER SIX
Eli, Mariah and Sophia Decide to Flee

When they were within minutes of their home, Eli called Mariah and asked her to open the garage door. Turning the corner, Eli pulled directly into the garage and quickly closed the garage door behind him.

Before Mariah could speak, Eli held up his hand, acknowledging her presence and alerting both Mariah and Sophia to be silent because he would say something momentarily. He quickly thought about the many years he had been with Mariah. She was steadfast in her support for him at his job and an excellent wife and mother. Sophia, like her mother, was a wonderful daughter. She excelled in her studies at the college where she was majoring in anthropology and archeology, and to his delight, she had become quite a linguist.

The beauty of both women was not superficial but extended deeply within their dispositions. He was driven to protect Mariah and Sophia and had already committed to doing whatever it would take to protect them.

Unconcerned for his own safety, Eli felt duty-bound as a husband and father to protect Mariah and Sophia from danger. *How am I going to tell them that our lives may be in threatened and that somehow Shamar might be unwittingly involved in this situation?*

He had never raised his voice before to Sophia, but today he had allowed a situation to get the better of him, and he had spoken to her harshly. Eli now spoke softly to both Sophia and Mariah. "Both of you please go to the living room."

Mariah was very uneasy as she put her arm around Sophia's waist and both hurried to the living room. Eli returned to the car to get the backpack.

Eli rushed to the living room and sat down, facing the two women. His expression was stern; it took several moments for him to compose himself and speak. Mariah could not remember a time when Eli had been this distressed.

"I have something that I need to share with both of you, and hopefully we can work on a solution together. You must understand that I believe our lives are in jeopardy." Both women looked at Eli in total surprise.

Sophia interjected, "Is Shamar in danger too? Is that why we examined the docks, because we were looking for Shamar?"

On the heels of Sophia's statement, Mariah interjected, "Eli, this is not like you. You are scaring us with your statements of danger. How could our lives be in danger?"

Eli gave a big sigh and continued in a slightly nervous voice, "I am sorry for being so cloak-and-dagger, but our lives are at stake. It is important that you do exactly what I tell you to do, including who you can talk to and who to trust. Believe me when I state that not only are we in danger, but I have also learned that some person or persons could resort to violence or worse against any of us, either individually or together." Eli could see the looks of fright on both their faces.

Eli continued, "I don't yet know who this someone is, but the rabbi's letters, which I had assumed were the rambling of an old man, I now understand were factual clues in a desperate attempt to hide his archeological findings from certain evil individuals.

"The person or persons the rabbi tried to warn me about will kill us to get what they want. I am uncertain of exactly what they are looking for, but it's clear the rabbi sent me something that has placed our lives in danger. This morning, I received a large envelope from New York. The return address was from an attorney. Enclosed were one letter and an envelope. The letter was from an attorney, and the sealed envelope was from the rabbi.

"I opened the rabbi's envelope first. I found in the sealed envelope from the rabbi two keys. One had a small tag attached to it, and the second key, which looked like it was crumbling from age, had no note attached to it." Eli took the keys from his pocket and placed them on the coffee table. "Then I read the attorney's informing telling me of the rabbi's death."

"Why would the rabbi send you two keys in a sealed envelope, Eli?" Mariah asked.

Eli quickly answered her. "Well, the note on one of the keys gives an address in the mountains to a cabin the rabbi has prepared so we can escape from danger long enough to compile the secret codes he sent to me in his letters.

"The rabbi's note also said that if I am reading this, he could not help me. His instructions to me were to reexamine the envelope, as he had sent a message written on the inside of the envelope. He stated that he had sent two items to me before meeting with his attorney, a robe and crate, and that he sent the items because he no longer trusted his lawyer. Clearly the rabbi knew something was awry. Nonetheless, I received the two packages from the rabbi last evening that he mentions in this letter. They were delivered to the docks.

"The rabbi also left me a phone message on my personal line instructing me to wear the robe in the red box before I opened the crate. I asked Shamar to go to the dock this morning to look for the crate and to wear the robe from the red box. He was to get back with me after securing the packages. Shamar called my secretary and stated he had the packages and that he would be up soon. As far as I can tell, Shamar followed my instructions. But Shamar never came to my office, and that was the last communication we had with him."

"That's why we checked the docks today; you knew Shamar was in danger," Sophia shouted.

Eli looked at both women and found no words to comfort them or explain his actions. He continued, "I fear that the rabbi may have been searching for the same religious relics that eventually caused Edward's death. I don't yet understand what this artifact is but I know religious artifacts are cherished due to their perceived spiritual abilities, and if that is the case, we are all in imminent danger, including Shamar.

"I was heading to the docks when Sophia arrived." Eli stopped speaking for a moment as he recalled the events of that morning. "Mariah, Sophia and I searched the docks for Shamar. At the docks I found several scraps of paper that were from a New York newspaper. The date at the top of the page was the same day the rabbi died. He mailed this information to me knowing the possibility of his death.

"I feel the need to protect my family and Shamar; however, I find myself very frustrated because I don't know what threatens us or how to protect us. I am worried for Shamar since someone believes the two items sent to me by the rabbi are valuable, perhaps precious enough to kill for."

Looking to Sophia and then back to Mariah, he continued. "Sophia, these were my thoughts while driving home; I don't understand certain pieces of information the rabbi doled out to me over the last six months; I believe we need to find Shamar and rescue him. This is a tall order, but I think between the three of us we will be successful.

"I'm going to need help from both of you; we must go through all correspondence from the rabbi and these scraps of paper." Eli began to empty his other pocket and placed the scraps of paper onto the coffee table.

Mariah looked at Sophia and then to Eli. "Eli, you did say Rabbi Katz?"

"Yes," he replied in a slightly questioning voice. "Do you remember him?"

Mariah waited for a moment and then replied, "Eli, the rabbi sent me some correspondence a few days ago. It arrived here at our home. It was a large yellow envelope. I understood from our phone conversation that I was to wait for a red box. I received the red box today by special carrier. As instructed, I was to wait for you, and you would know when to open the red box. Eli, I thought the rabbi was sending you something special for the museum."

Sophia asked, "Why was Rabbi Katz so mysterious about this crate and robe, and why would he be sending information to Mom and asking that she keep it secret?"

To Eli's surprise, Mariah began to answer Sophia. "During the rabbi's phone conversation, he stated that he was very impressed with our family. He thought of your father not just as a good friend but also as a son—a son he was proud of.

"The rabbi realized the box and his information needed to be in a secure place, so he sent them directly to you and to our home. He was on his way to the synagogue, and so our conversation was short."

"Let's go see what he sent then," Eli said, hurrying up the stairs.

Mariah set the box on a dressing table and opened it. To their astonishment, they beheld a beautiful red robe embroidered in gold and silver markings in what appeared to be a snake. Eli reached out to embrace both Mariah and Sophia. All were startled as the front door bell rang, and Mariah instinctively moved closer to Sophia. Both women looked to Eli. The expression on Eli's face revealed that he too was taken by surprise.

He slowly stood up and softly instructed the women, "Be quiet and stay seated; I'll answer the door. Mariah, please put the scraps of paper and keys in your pocket."

Walking to the front door, Eli felt a surge of apprehension. Pausing for a moment, he wiped sweat from his brow. Opening the door, Eli was surprised to see Patrick standing on his doorstep.

Eli had never cared for this spoiled and selfish individual, especially after his father's death. Eli just wanted him to go away.

Before Eli could say anything, Patrick began to speak. "Hello, Eli. I apologize for the intrusion, but I feel I must let you know what happened at the museum docks early this morning."

Patrick began to move forward to enter Eli's home. Eli placed a firm hand on Patrick's chest, blocking his entrance into his home.

Patrick stopped speaking and slowly stepped back from Eli. He gave a tilt of his head to Eli, acknowledging Eli's request to stay upon the front step and not enter his home. His face showed surprise and annoyance at Eli's action. However, he could tell from Eli's stance that he meant business. Eli listened as Patrick resumed speaking.

"I sent several of my men to the docks to ensure that certain items that had been shipped to me from New York had arrived. I was informed that my package had arrived late last night at the museum docks.

"My men observed a man on the dock who they interpreted as stealing my shipment, so they reacted by beating the man up. After securing my items, they tried to make sure the man was OK, but he was gone. I feel badly for the actions of my men and came to apologize and pay for any medical expenses."

Eli stared at Patrick, choosing his words very carefully. While slowly closing the front door, Eli said, "Yes, injuries occurred on the museum dock today. However, the hospital has not yet told me about the bill. Patrick, please never send any of your workmen to my museum again. If you are expecting anything or wish to examine anything, contact me first.

"Thank you for your concern and for taking the time to inform me. Your timing is poor, as my family and I are gathering for a quiet evening together. If I need to contact you, I have your number. Good night."

"Wait!" Patrick shouted quickly. "Please, for just a moment. I promise it will be worth your while." Eli finished shutting the door. Patrick raised his voice, speaking through the closed door, "I have come to apologize for my actions since my father's death, Eli. I understand what a challenge I have been, and I am truly sorry. I came not only to apologize but to ask your help with an item I received at the docks today. It was an item my father was searching for before his death. Will you please accept my apology and help me?"

Eli had completely locked the deadbolt, locked the door handle, and connected the chain in its slot. Eli stood motionless behind the closed door, listening to Patrick's rambling and also listening as his footsteps slowly faded away on the pavement. Next he heard Patrick's car engine and then the sound of his car as it pulled away. The mystery had just become even stranger. Why was Patrick expecting a delivery at the museum docks? Was it a just a coincidence?

Eli returned to the living room, walking slowly toward his chair; then, looking at his wife and daughter, he chose to sit between them on the couch. Placing his arms around both of them, he gave each a kiss on the cheek and continued. "Something bad happened today, and I will do whatever it takes to protect both of you and Shamar. I'm sure you heard what Patrick said. I must admit I am very concerned. We must use the utmost caution with Patrick."

Mariah and Sophia leaned forward over the coffee table and continued to carefully open the crumbled scraps of paper while Eli spoke to them. They had decided to get one step ahead of Eli by finding and deciphering the crumbled notes the rabbi had sent.

Eli watched them unfolding the scraps while he continued. "However, here is what is the most disconcerting to me. I never received a call from a hospital about any of our employees being hurt on the docks, and no one notified me of an altercation on the docks. I sent Shamar to get a crate for me, and now I have not heard back from him or heard from him, which is totally out of character for Shamar. I don't understand why he might have been beaten or where he could have escaped to."

Eli paused momentarily, looking at Sophia, who had just taken in a deep breath of surprise. He watched as tears rolled from her eyes and down her cheeks. "Oh my Shamar," was her soft response.

Eli moved from the couch to get a box of tissues. He placed the box between the women. Eli watched as Mariah moved closer to Sophia and placed her arm around her shoulders. Both were visibly upset, and Eli once again comprehended how much Shamar meant to Sophia. Of all the men she had gone out with over the past few years, Eli agreed that Shamar was one of her best choices. Shamar was polite and an excellent student and worker, and Sophia appeared to be preoccupied with his science. Sophia loved to listen to him explain various theories to her.

The room remained silent for several moments; the only sound was the occasional sniffle from Sophia. Continuing his thoughts, Eli began to speak again. "I did find evidence that a fight took place. However, I was never told what happened, when it happened, or who was involved. I'm positive Patrick knows more about the docks than he is telling us. I believe that is why he showed up here; it was a fishing expedition. He might be pretending to apologize just to get our confidence and answers for something he's working on."

Sophia interrupted her father. "Patrick asked me out to breakfast this morning, and I turned him down. He stated that he had something he wanted to share with me and he was sure I would find it very interesting. I just feel so uncomfortable around him, and I didn't want to waste my day with someone I dislike. Besides, I promised Shamar I would help with the displays he was preparing. We were going to work together on the staging of an exhibit."

Eli said, "Patrick mentioned a crate; do you think he has knowledge of the robe and crate? How did he know about my shipment from the rabbi? If so, who told him what time it would be delivered and where? There are too many coincidences, and in light of everything else going on, I am really concerned."

Sophia said, "Father, what was it that you noticed on the docks, and what do you think happened?"

Eli looked at Sophia and Mariah, "I noticed some blood on the dock and knew someone had been hurt. I didn't know who was hurt until Patrick came to our home. I have had no communication from a hospital, which may indicate Shamar was not seriously injured. Perhaps that is why he has not called us. Or maybe he passed out. We need to find him."

Eli continued, "Patrick's inquiry is more than a little odd. He came here because he wants information. I'm concerned about Patrick's involvement in this—not only because he knew about the crates but because he has a reputation for strong-arming his way to get what he wants."

Eli decided they should leave as soon as possible. Turning toward the women, he instructed them, "Pack one suitcase each. We need to be ready to leave within the next hour. Sophia, make sure you have all the information you believe we need so we can work together deciphering clues within the rabbi's letters. I'm going to prepare the house and car for our trip. The cabin does not have all the necessities we have here, so pack accordingly. Mariah, please pack one suitcase with food items. The cabin has plates, dishes, silverware, bedding, and towels, and that is about it. We need enough food for perhaps two weeks."

Heading to the garage to begin preparing the car for their trip, Eli observed a young man peeking in the front window. He was trying to hide himself but was not good at concealment. Panic ran through Eli as his adrenalin ran high. His instinct to protect his family overrode his senses of caution and reason. Running to the front door, Eli rushed out of the house and continued at a fast pace toward the man, who was now standing by the window.

The man did not move as he saw Eli charging toward him. Eli grabbed the man by the front of his shirt and swung his fist, striking the young man squarely on the jaw. As the young man began to get up, Eli asked, "Who are you, and what are you doing here?"

Before the young man could answer, Eli took another swing with his fist. The young man blocked the second swing and in an angry voice stated, "I'm not here to hurt you or your family. I have come to warn you to be cautious of Patrick. My name is Gabriel, and Addison told me where you live so I could warn you."

Eli asked, "Who sent you, and why are you at my window?"

Gabriel stated that he had taken a box containing a crate from the museum and that Patrick needed to have Sophia decipher things that were supposed to be written on or within that crate. Gabriel continued, "Patrick was very upset when Sophia declined his invitation to breakfast. When I took the crate to Patrick, I watched his whole demeanor change. I panicked with fear at what I saw happening before me, but I was so frightened that I couldn't run. I was alarmed enough that I spoke to Addison and my mother spoke to me, and both of them had only words of concern to share with me. Because of these conversations, I have decided to quit working for Patrick. But I was so scared by Patrick's transformation when he touched that crate that I chose to warn you and your family."

Eli slowly released his hold on Gabriel. Politely Eli asked Gabriel, "What kind of transformation took place that scared you? Did the crate change?"

Gabriel was quick to answer. "Oh, it was Patrick, sir. His face changed to something sinister, and his hands shook the closer they got to the crate."

Sophia rushed from the front door to where Eli and Gabriel were. She was surprised to see that her father had had an altercation with Gabriel. She also noticed that Gabriel's lip was split and bleeding, "Father, what have you done?" she said, scolding her father.

Gabriel said, "Hello, Sophia. I've come to warn you."

Eli turned his head to Sophia and asked, "You know this man?"

"I don't really know him, but I know of him and that he works for Patrick and has always been very kind to me."

Sophia continued, "Father, we must go inside as quickly as possible, and Gabriel, you must come too. Both of you march right now into the kitchen, and I don't want to hear a word out of either of you." Both men looked at each other and then silently followed Sophia inside the house.

Mariah was standing in the living room and said, "Oh my God," when she saw Gabriel's face. "Follow me," were her next words. Gabriel and Eli followed Mariah from the living room into the kitchen. Sophia grabbed the first-aid kit, and the women began to clean Gabriel's wound.

Eli watched as the women cleaned the wounds and began to ask questions, "Gabriel, I am sorry that I punched you, but I thought you were someone who might hurt my family. You said you took a crate to Patrick at his home. Can you tell me more about the crate? Where did you find the crate, and how did you know where to find it?"

Gabriel replied, "Patrick sent me and two of my men to the museum to retrieve his box. After I found the crate, I called Patrick, and he asked me to bring it to his mansion."

"The museum," began Eli. "Where in the museum would you find Patrick's box?"

Gabriel seemed delighted to answer Eli. "We searched throughout the museum, and not finding the box, we went to the loading dock, and there on the dock was a man opening Patrick's box, so my men beat the man and asked him questions. That man crawled off into a corner, and I don't know what happened to him. My men and I took the box containing his crate to Patrick's home."

Eli thought for a moment and asked another question. "Gabriel, what did this man look like? How was he dressed, how tall was he, and what color was his hair?"

Stillness hung over the kitchen as Eli, Mariah, and Sophia anxiously anticipated Gabriel's answer. To their surprise, Gabriel quickly answered. "He was dressed like a monk, He was wearing a black robe, had blond hair, and I would guess his height to be maybe five foot ten or eleven."

Sophia gasped as she heard the answer. Turning her back to everyone, Sophia walked to the kitchen sink. Mariah immediately went to Sophia and held her daughter.

Gabriel could see that his information had struck at Sophia's heart. Meekly he turned to Eli and in a hushed voice asked, "Who was the man on the dock?"

Eli answered in a soft voice, "Her boyfriend, Shamar."

Feeling very bad about his actions on the docks, and seeing the pain it was causing Sophia, Gabriel stood up and said out loud, "I'm very sorry, Sophia. This is why I choose to no longer work for Patrick. Please forgive me. If there is anything I can do or any way I can help, just ask." Gabriel thanked everyone for their help and quickly left.

Eli walked up to the women and placed his arms around both of them. He said, "We need to accelerate our packing and leave as quickly as possible. Gabriel shed some light on our situation; he reemphasized that we must be cautious of Patrick, and now we know why Patrick wanted to have breakfast with you, Sophia—so you could decipher a crate for him. I am going to prepare the house as if we are vacationing. Please remember to pack all that you think we will need, and do it as quickly as possible."

Returning to the living room, Eli activated automatic timers on the television, radio, and various lamps.

The women had finished packing all they thought was needed and placed the suitcases at the entry to the garage door. Eli joined them in the kitchen. Sophia was still very sad, and Eli didn't know what to say.

Finally Mariah broke the silence. "I think we are ready, Eli. How about you?"

The phone rang, and everyone froze for a moment. Eli said, "Let it go to the answering machine."

Everyone waited for the machine to kick on, exposing who had called. After the fourth ring, the machine came on, to their surprise, it was Addison. Eli rushed to the phone and picked it up. He and Addison talked for a few moments.

When the call was done, Eli erased all messages. He turned to the women and said, "Let's go," and the women began to walk to the garage. Eli placed the suitcases in the car and jumped into the driver's seat. Opening the garage door, Eli pulled the car out onto the street, and they began their journey into the mountains.

CHAPTER SEVEN
Sago is Introduced

Arriving at his high-rise apartment, Sago paused, waiting for the door to be opened. He turned to his driver, saying, "I will need a ride later this evening. Have the car stocked with refreshments and drinks."

The doorman rushed to open the limousine door and said, "Good day, Mr. Kragulijac." A second high-rise assistant opened the front door of the building, also greeting Mr. Kragulijac in the same slave-like manner.

Sago walked to the elevator, entered, and pushed the penthouse button. The ride was quick. When the elevator doors opened, his butler greeted him. "Good day, sir. I shall have your refreshment prepared at the terrace as instructed."

"Very good," replied Sago.

Walking into his office, Sago strolled to his desk and sat down. He opened a drawer and placed three files face up in front of him. Sago moved each file in various positions and then placed them side by side. He said out loud as he touched each file, "Eli, Mariah, and Addison."

He deliberated each file, pondering when and why a connection had been formed with the late Rabbi Katz. As he touched and moved each file around, he thought to himself, *where did you meet the rabbi, and what did the rabbi tell you? Why did the rabbi choose these individuals?* So far his investigator had only linked all four with each other through an archeological dig in Alexandria, Egypt.

Pushing his chair away from the desk, Sago commenced pacing in front of the fire place. His thoughts continued to swirl regarding why Eli had been in communication with the rabbi for nearly three years, although Eli had never made any public acknowledgment that a relationship existed between them.

My informants found nothing connecting Eli to any research on the crystal and have confirmed more of a companionship than a joint venture with the rabbi. Could Eli be uninformed, or is he exceptionally good at hiding what he knows?

Shifting his thoughts to the other files, Sago walked closer to his desk and looked down at Mariah's file and tapped on it. Mariah, as far as Sago knew, had had no communication with the rabbi other than at social events. Naturally she would be gracious to all guests attending a social event at the museum, since that was her nature.

His thoughts continued. *However, both Mariah and Eli assisted Edward at his dig in Alexandria some years ago.* No details about that assistance had appeared in any writings that Sago had uncovered.

Perhaps the rabbi was just a contributor to the museum, but why did he send the crate and a red box to Eli? What was this mysterious robe with regard to the rabbi, and how did the rabbi come into its possession? Who is this Shamar who was wearing the robe?

If I eliminate Eli and Mariah, that leaves only Addison, the butler Edward confided in. He is old school and very loyal to his deceased employer. Also, Addison traveled to Alexandria with Edward. Possibly this is where I should direct my inquiries—to the butler.

Sago carefully examined each file again, to be familiar with each individual and his or her psychological boundaries. Sago had chosen to step up his investigation of each person so he would be very knowledgeable about their strengths, weaknesses, fears, and vulnerabilities.

He was especially interested in their breaking points. "I shall push each individual's emotions, forcing them beyond their physical or mental endurance to the ultimate breakdown or death, and I don't really care which comes first. I want and will obtain what I desire."

Picking up his phone, Sago dialed the familiar number. "Hello, Darby, this is Sago, and I require a job done immediately. I want the findings back to me very quickly. I must have the home of the late Rabbi Katz entered into. I want video and pictures of each room, video and pictures of each drawer, video and pictures of each wall, video and pictures of the floor—absolutely everything in his home photographed and videoed. Have one of your assistants formulate a diagram with exact dimensions, and compare that drawing with those filed at the city hall. I must know if any alterations were ever made to his home.

"I also want Eli Daniels's house, Patrick's mansion, Addison's quarters, and Shamar's apartment videotaped and photographed in the same manner. I need the results of your investigation very quickly. Also I need some of your men to examine the attorney's office and his home. I don't want any evidence that you were at any of those places. This must be a stealth project, and I expect top priority over anything else you are working on."

Sago hung up the phone and turned to look out the plate glass doors onto his terrace. His mind was weighing the possibilities before progressing forward.

Sago walked over to his filing area and gathered a new file folder. Using a three-hole punch, he pierced several sheets of paper. Next he secured a new file folder and placed the pierced sheets inside it. He collected the envelope from his investigation and then sat down at his desk. In bold letters he printed S-H-A-M-A-R on the side tab of the file. Opening the envelope, he began to enter information from the investigator's report into the file.

Sago evaluated the information gathered on Shamar.
1. He is studying physics and is a good student.
2. He likes Sophia Daniels, daughter of Eli Daniels, and at the present helps stage exhibits at the library where Eli is curator.
3. He found no ties with anyone connected to the crate or archeological expeditions.
4. He was at the docks and in the process of retrieving a crate for Eli. A red box was noted by his investigator; however, the red box, in conjunction with the crate, is still somewhat mysterious.
5. Shamar had put on the robe that was in the red box. Robe is missing. Further investigation of crate and red box indicates these items were sent to the museum by Rabbi Katz to Eli Daniels.

Other than that one act at the docks by Shamar, Sago could not find anything connecting him to the rabbi. Sago's interest was piqued, and he became curious about how Shamar might be involved.

Sago closed Shamar's folder, picked up the phone again, and pushed redial. "I need you to do one more thing for me. Go to Patrick's home and ask for Addison. I have already placed a questionnaire in his mailbox, and I want you to tell him you are investigating or following up on the missing pieces from the Alexandria dig several years ago. Carry an investigator's badge and statements from other witnesses who were working the site at the time the pieces were discovered to be missing. I must know what Addison recalls and how detailed his memory remains. I need this information promptly." Sago hung up the phone.

Sago pulled from the desk drawer the notebook Darby had taken from Rabbi Katz's home shortly after killing him. He gave a quick look at the chapters.

1. At chapter one, he found a discussion about dragons and snakes, along with something about small scrolls. This short story was uninteresting and lacked clarity. It seemed to be just rambling.
2. He narrated a short story about the Library of Alexandria. Again uninteresting.
3. The rabbi felt that the library was ahead of its time, remarkable as astrologist and philosophy enthusiasts survived the changes between ideologies and religions.
4. A quote written by the rabbi read, "There have been too many fires, earthquakes, and destructive takeovers that have destroyed not just the great library and its vast knowledge but that which was once, beyond a doubt, the greatest research and learning facility the world has ever known."

Sago's thoughts drifted back to Eli, Mariah, and Addison. *I must come to a decision about Eli, Mariah, and Addison. Are they aware of what the rabbi wrote in his journal, and do they understand what it refers to?* Sago looked down at the rabbi's highlighted notes in the outer column of his journal regarding Ptolemy. Sago reconsidered and came to the conclusion that he was missing something, *But what, and how can it keep eluding me?*

Sago went to another section of his file cabinet. He removed several files and began to pile them up on the top of his file cabinet. When he had pulled out all he wanted, he paused and then picked up the phone, requesting that the butler fire up the outdoor fireplace.

Opening the plate glass doors, Sago walked out onto his well-manicured terrace. Moving toward the border, he hesitated briefly and then continued walking the length of the border, viewing the city around and below him. Turning to the table and chairs, he sat down. His butler arrived with refreshments, placing them on the table, and then immediately began the fire in the outdoor fireplace. No words were exchanged between them, and the butler quickly exited back into the manor.

As Sago sipped his coffee, he mentally reviewed his last five years of searching. He considered what the rabbi had gathered and written in his journal, yet he remained puzzled about the writing and what it was supposed to mean.

Occasionally, he wondered whether the rabbi might have had dementia while composing his journal. Sago desired to grasp and understand what he knew was either missing or hidden by the rabbi. *But who could translate the gibberish?*

Finishing his refreshment, Sago gathered the files and took them to the fire. One by one, he reexamined the name on the file before tossing it into the fire to be destroyed. Each of these individuals he had a file on had been interviewed and terminated.

When he held Edward's file in his hand, he could not resist the urge to read once more how Edward had passed away. How clever, he marveled, that his assistants had thought to infect Edward with a disease that only an archeologist could come into contact with on a dig. It made his death even more believable.

The butler arrived with a tray that held a telegram. Sago retrieved the message and read its contents. Soon a smile of delight crossed his face. The butler was waiting for a response from Sago, who looked to the butler and said, "Bring the car around. I will be gone for a while. When I return, have all of this ash removed and disposed of. If something does not burn, make sure it is rekindled and destroyed."

For Sago the trip and time seemed to pass slowly. However, it gave him time to think of what his next move should be. "How sweet," he said out loud, "a new opportunity has been placed before me." Patrick had contacted Sago and informed him that he had uncovered information Sago was seeking.

Clever Edward had built an underground bunker and had told no one of its existence except Addison. Patrick was certain that Addison knew not only about the bunker but also what it held. "Patrick had better be right this time," Sago mumbled out loud.

CHAPTER EIGHT

Eli, Mariah and Sophia Drive to the Mountains

As soon as the car left the driveway and they were headed down the street, Mariah said, "Eli, I think it is time you told Sophia and me what the rabbi shared with you and what Addison wanted. Obviously it is important because you are concealing something from us."

Eli hesitated before answering. "Patrick has no clue as to the potential perils of that crate, especially if it is the same crate Edward was searching for. However, you and I *do,* Mariah. I remember some of what Edward mentioned to me while we were in Alexandria about that crate. Some of the things he said to me seemed weird, and I thought Edward was relying too much on the rumors about the crate. I believed Edward needed more facts before acting on what seemed like superstitious ramblings. But there are enough unexplainable discoveries that we can't ignore them."

"What Edward stumbled onto must be of great significance for people to take such extreme measures to learn about it and then cover it up," Mariah interjected. "I was always concerned about the extent of death, deception, and effort associated with the search for information concerning this particular artifact. And I've always wondered about the source and basis for the rumors about the crate."

"Yes," added Eli. "A greater worry for me, and to Addison as well, was who—who continued searching for the crate with wanton disregard for the lives sacrificed, sometimes for insignificantly small bits of new information? And now we wonder whether those involved present a threat to our family and to Shamar. It is likely that they do because they think we know something or have something they need."

Mariah then asked, "So you think there might be someone other than Patrick searching for this chest? Perhaps someone has enticed Patrick in such a clever way that he doesn't realize he's being used. If that's so, Patrick will become a liability as soon as the chest is found. Patrick does not realize his very existence is in danger."

Sophia then asked, "Does anyone know who, besides Patrick, could be searching for the chest? It would seem that over the years the person searching would have left clues as to where and why he was searching."

Eli said, "The rabbi mentioned to me the *one* but never placed a name with his theory. I believe the *one* is a very dangerous individual obsessed with this crate."

Mariah asked, "What did Addison want?"

Eli answered, "Addison is concerned about Patrick. He said that lately Patrick has been acting unusual. When Patrick opened the *crate* today, they saw three magnificent glass flasks. When holding one of them, Patrick behaved very oddly and claimed to have a strange vision, and he had a burning look in his eyes."

"Could that be what Gabriel witnessed?" Mariah exclaimed excitedly. "Was that the transformation he saw?"

Eli answered Mariah, "I don't know, but I think what Gabriel saw was something different." Eli slowly continued, "When Addison viewed the last flask, one in which he could see numerous scrolls, a voice whispered to him that Patrick was possessed by an evil being. He also added that Patrick had strange visions and odd sensations when he held the first two flasks."

Sophia said, "Let me confirm what I think you are explaining to us—that the burning around Patrick's eyes was caused by an entity within the flask attempting to pull the evil from Patrick?"

Eli answered, "Yes," and then slowly asked Sophia, "What about the other vision? Patrick said he did not recognize the voice calling to him."

Sophia leaned forward from the backseat. "If the third flask was informing Addison that the first two flasks were attempting to help Patrick, then we could have a serious problem.

"Consider these circumstances: the snake and dragon recognized the evil, and they knew how to deal with it, but the evil within Patrick was so strong that these two together could not restrain or remove the evil. Now we've been added to the mix, and how are we to accomplish the task of removing evil from Patrick?"

In a soft voice, Eli said, "We need to find clues in the rabbi's correspondence because I do not know the answer."

Mariah said, "Eli, you are talking of possession and evil so calmly that it frightens me. Is this evil after us? They think we know something, don't they? Or they think we have something, correct?"

Turning in her seat so Sophia and Eli could both hear her, Mariah continued. "This is because we helped Edward with that dig in Alexandria, isn't it?" Sophia and Eli could hear the fear building up as Mariah continued. "Well I don't like the situation we are in. I think that when we stop for gas, we should also get some disposable phones, and we need code words to use with each other so we will know if we are in trouble."

Eli quickly responded, "I hope the answers will be in the scraps of paper the rabbi sent to us, as well as some of the things he said to me." Eli did not address the other questions Mariah had asked.

Mariah spoke up in a softer tone. "I never understood why Patrick's father continued searching for the crate even after all that took place in Alexandria. Now I believe he was trying to protect his family and himself from an evil being—an evil being that might now be after us."

Sophia cut her mother short. "I don't understand all that both of you are referring to concerning Alexandria, Egypt. However, I remember Edward and his obsession with a quest he was working on, and I remember Patrick complaining that he and his mother hardly saw him, even when he was home. Am I correct in understanding that the crate was his obsession? Would someone please fill me in on anything else I am missing?"

Mariah answered Sophia's question. "I don't know how Edward found out about this crate, but he did, and it became his driving force until the day he died. Rose and Patrick rarely interacted with Edward because he was so consumed with finding the crate. Your father and I went with Edward to the dig in Alexandria because Edward thought he knew where to find what he was searching for. We thought we were helping put an end to his great, consuming quest and freeing him from this obsession that was dividing him from his family.

"While in Alexandria, Edward helped with a particular dig near Pompey's Pillar that later proved to be the end of Edward's career. Edward, your father, and I were discussing a particular item found that afternoon at Pompey's Pillar over dinner. None of us could agree on a description of a particular item that was found, each of us remembered the item a little differently, so we all decided to go to the holding area and reexamine that unique piece. To our surprise and dismay, the item was missing. This was a very bad situation for Edward.

"Naturally Edward was held accountable for the loss. Your father and I tried to convince the board that Edward had nothing to do with the disappearance of any items, and that he was not hiding anything, but the board was livid, and Edward was not allowed access to any sites for a number of years."

Eli added, "After the board's decision, Edward became a recluse, feeling he had let his family, the museum, and himself down. He took up gardening and built that beautiful area in their courtyard."

Mariah said, "Addison remained close to Edward. As a matter of fact, Addison was arriving at the site in Alexandria the same day Eli and I left. Edward knew he could trust Addison and feared what the board's decision would be about the missing pieces. That was their last visit to Alexandria and any archeological site."

Mariah saw a sign for a truck stop and asked Eli to stop for gas and disposable telephones. Eli responded, "I also want to stop at an ATM at the airport to get cash. I want people to believe we were there and used the machine to get cash to go the rabbi's funeral."

Sophia and Mariah both looked slightly confused, and Sophia said, "Shouldn't we be heading out of town and not to the airport? There are plenty of ATMs between here and the mountains that we can use."

"Let me explain something to each of you," Eli began in a raised voice. "I don't think anyone knows about the rabbi's hideaway. My secretary believes we are attending a funeral in New York. This ruse may allow us time to study the rabbi's letters and vital information and clues. We cannot take the chance and use credit cards. We must use cash only. We must leave no money trail that can be followed. I am certain professional hit men are after us, and we must do all we can to protect our location at all times. I like Mariah's idea of disposable cell phones to communicate with each other in case we get separated, but I don't like the idea of using ATMs and leaving a trail."

Everyone was quiet after that, and Eli continued after a short pause. "Whoever is searching for us must believe we are in New York." Eli looked in his rearview mirror to the backseat to see if Sophia was OK. She looked so sad and worried. This only added to his guilt. He wondered whether she would forgive him if something had happened to Shamar.

They pulled into the truck stop to gas up and purchase disposable cell phones. Eli handed Mariah some cash and asked her to put all of it on pump five and said he would gas up the car while they purchased disposable cell phones. "Don't use credit cards," he said as they walked into the truck stop's main store.

The women returned, and Eli distributed the phones and began driving again, this time to the airport. After a short while, they were nearing the airport terminal, and Eli began to advise Mariah where she might find ATMs. Eli pulled up to the drop-off zone and told Mariah he would circle around and come back for her. Mariah jumped out of the car and headed into the terminal.

Mariah entered the airport terminal and followed the signs directing people up the stairs to the lounges, ticket counter, and ATM. She was considering how much she should take out of the savings account and how much to get from the checking account.

Slowing her pace, she allowed the two men approaching the escalator to go ahead of her. As the men continued their conversation, Mariah stepped on the escalator behind them. Soon she realized they were talking about her and Eli.

The older man was instructing the younger on how to get information from the ticket agent so they would know which flight to take to New York. "Watch a pro and see how it is done," he said to the younger man.

The discussion continued about her and Eli and how they must get the same travel arrangements to New York as the Daniels family.

Mariah became frightened. As she began to step off the escalator, she saw the men approaching the ticket counter. Nervously she stepped off the escalator and began to glance around for not only an ATM but a possible escape route too.

She slowed her pace, looking up as if reading the signs to various places, when in actuality she was listening to the men speak to the ticket agent. Moving closer to the men, she continued to listen to their conversation.

The little voice in her head began to instruct her to keep going toward the ATM, get the money, and stick with the family plan; however, another part of her wanted to know who these people were, how they knew their names, and how they had found out about the Daniels attending a funeral in New York.

Her sensible, frightened side took over, and she casually strolled off in another direction away from the men. She saw the ATM and continued in that direction.

Reaching the ATM, she opened her purse and took out her card. She inserted the card and ignored the instructions because she was watching the men's reflections on the monitor. Finally she began the task of retrieving money from the machine. After getting money from both accounts, Mariah stopped and watched the men in the reflection. There were now five men gathered together speaking to each other.

Although she wanted to run, she continued to walk. Not wanting to draw any attention to herself, she strolled toward a concession stand and stared at some pretty scarves. The stand was located in an area within hearing range of the men who were now gathered at a small table to have a drink.

They were double-checking who was to be at the departure gates and parking garage and who had tickets for various flights to New York. It seemed the airline would not give information due to a privacy act; however, they did sell them tickets for each flight. All one-way tickets, of course.

Mariah learned from the conversation that these men had the license plate number to their car and that a man named Darby made sure the attorney had notified Eli of the rabbi's death.

Overpowering fear was starting to take over Mariah's rational mind. She thought that if anyone recognized her, they would kill her. What about the car? They had the license plate and description, and if she got back into the car, they would all be killed. Trying to formulate an escape plan, Mariah purchased a scarf and turned toward the escalator. She noticed the men at the counter had turned to look in her direction. She paused for a moment and then thought to herself, *don't look or act suspicious. Just keep moving.*

Reaching the escalator, she grasped the rubber rail and began to move down the stairs. Two of the men were behind her. Her heart was pounding, and small sweat beads were forming on her brow. She was trying to think of something clever to do. All she could come up with was to search for a bathroom. She saw something out of the corner of her eye, and as soon as the step reached the floor level, she darted in the direction of the ladies room. The men also exited the escalator; however, they split up, with one going toward the parking garage and the other stepping outside to smoke a cigarette.

Reaching the bathroom, she rushed inside and took the first stall. She was fumbling in her purse for the disposable phone to warn Eli and Sophia. Panic and anxiety triggered an even deeper nervousness. She fumbled in her purse, trying to pull out a cell phone, but her fingers were so incapacitated by panic that she couldn't function.

She paused, totally lost as to what she should do; hastily she left the ladies room. Mariah rushed out the doors to the street, seeking shelter. Anxiously she hailed a cab. Unaware of her surroundings, Mariah was functioning on adrenalin.

She could only recall the prearranged meeting area. Mariah was filled with fear and thought to herself, *What if one of them recognizes me? I could put my entire family in danger.* She never even looked for Eli or Sophia, who were circling the parking lot.

Mariah quickly entered the cab, instructing the driver to take her to the museum and to please drive around awhile before getting there. "I just met an old school chum and want to lose him. Would you please make sure we are not followed?"

The short circling of the airport took almost ten minutes to complete. Sophia and Eli returned to the spot where they had dropped Mariah off. She was not there. Sophia offered to go inside and find her, but Eli said no. "We will circle again, and if Mariah is not here, we will park, go inside, and find her."

Eli slowly pulled away from the curb, watching his rearview mirror. When he returned his attention to the road, he slammed on his brakes. Two men were crossing in the crosswalk in front of them. He was grateful he had not hit them. Both men were pulling suitcases behind them and obviously were not in a hurry. Eli wished they would move faster.

Sophia glanced behind her and yelled, "Stop, Father, stop. Mom's right behind us."

Looking into the rear mirror, Eli saw Mariah exiting the terminal. She was not approaching the car. At first Eli thought she didn't see the car, and he was preparing to honk the horn when he and Sophia witnessed something that caused them a great deal of concern. Mariah was hailing a cab.

Eli's heart raced, and he heard Sophia exclaim, "What is she doing?"

A yellow cab pulled up, and Mariah entered its backseat. Eli and Sophia were unprepared for this twist of plans. Eli watched as the taxi slowly passed by.

Sophia jumped from the backseat into the front passenger seat, yelling at her father, "Follow that cab!"

Eli's instincts kicked in, and he locked the car doors and placed the master lock in place so Sophia couldn't exit the car. "No, Sophia," he said, "We cannot and will not follow the cab. Your mother knows what she is doing, and right now we must trust her judgment. My guess is that something happened and she is trying to protect us. We will wait for her at the prearranged destination."

Sophia pulled her cell phone from her pocket. Eli grabbed the phone and placed it in his breast pocket. In a firm voice, he said, "*No*, no Sophia. You cannot contact your mother, especially by cell phone. This is hard for both of us, but we must wait for her to contact us. If we contact her, we may be making a serious mistake. I'm worried too, but I trust your mother and will wait for her to contact us. We each know the prearranged meeting place and the passwords for communicating."

Both watched as the taxi disappeared down the road, headed toward downtown Denver. Eli looked around to see if anyone was watching, but he noticed nothing unusual. Slowly Eli pulled away. He needed to think, but he was too distraught to concentrate. He was alarmed that Mariah had acted as she had, but he understood Mariah wouldn't do this unless it were an absolute necessity. A dark thought passed through his mind, sending a wave of gloom throughout his body.

Sophia's fright had welled up inside of her, and she began to cry. "Daddy, we must do something. We must help Mother." Eli put on a false smile and grasped Sophia's hand. "She will call us, Sophia. She will call us. We need to be patient. She loves us and will do nothing to let us down."

The Thirteenth Stone of Aaron

Eli and Sophia drove in silence to the prearranged meeting place, each suppressing their thoughts and fears. When they pulled into the gas station's parking area, Eli thought Mariah had picked the perfect place to park and hide.

This gas station was on a corner, somewhat secluded from anything else. The station was centered in a U-shaped parking area. Enclosing all three sides of the gas station were tall evergreens that protected a parking area that provided visibility of all persons walking by, entering, or leaving the station.

Eli backed the car into a parking space and then turned off the lights and waited. He and Sophia anxiously waited for Mariah to contact them. Eli checked his watch repeatedly, wondering whether Mariah was OK, what was happening, and what he was going to do!

How long would he wait? As the time passed, Eli recognized that he must decide whether he should go to the cabin without Mariah or continue to wait. He chose to wait awhile longer.

Eli had gone inside the gas station for coffee, and as he was returning to the car, Sophia jumped out, excitedly proclaiming, "She is all right. She said she will meet us here in about fifteen minutes. She texted me and asked if we were OK at our special place, and I told her yes."

Eli was relieved at the news but wondered if Mariah had used the secret passwords they had prearranged. Eli asked Sophia, "Did she use the secret password? Are you sure it was from your mother and not someone else?"

Sophia answered, "Yes, she used the password. She will be arriving in a few moments with my car."

Eli looked at Sophia. "Your car? How did she get your car?"

Mariah arrived and parked Sophia's car a short distance from Eli's. She ran up to Eli and grabbed him, holding Eli tightly in her arms. Quickly releasing Eli, Mariah began to jabber excitedly, drowning out her voice. She said, "I'll explain later, but we need to continue with our plans and escape without delay. You lead the way, and Sophia and I will follow."

Eli was shocked and concerned at Mariah's state of mind. He placed his arms around Mariah and said, "I am so glad you are OK, but you must tell me what happened. I'm not going to just drive off into the mountains without an explanation." Softly he whispered, "I was so frightened, Mariah, I thought something bad had happened, but I am glad that you are OK."

Eli was thinking while he looked into Mariah's eyes. Mariah, seeing the concern upon Eli's face, gently kissed his cheek, and without the stress or excitement in her voice said, "Eli, you were so right about thugs wanting to get to us. At the airport, I overheard a conversation concerning us, and I struggled to keep what self-control I had. There's perhaps five or six detective-like men searching for us, and they knew we were headed to New York for a funeral. They also know the license plate on your car, Eli, and someone named Darby sent similar or the same men to the attorney's office and instructed the attorney to send you the letter you received about the rabbi's death.

"Eli, while you were packing the car, Sophia and I agreed that we need two vehicles, so I went to the museum and got Sophia's car. I believe it is important that neither of us be placed in a position where we can become stranded, and having our own transportation will give us the capability to separate when needed and the ability to meet again at a predetermined spot."

Eli thought about what Mariah said had happened at the airport. Then he answered Mariah. "Yes, you are right that we need two cars, so let's make sure Sophia's car has been gassed up, and then we'll go to the mountains." Eli was torn about separating from Sophia and Mariah to make the long trip into the mountains.

Looking at Mariah, Eli asked, "Mariah, why did you take a cab?"

She replied, "Eli, these men knew your license plate number. I didn't want to take a chance, just in case I was seen or recognized, so I decided to catch a cab. Then I went to the museum to get Sophia's car."

Eli felt awkward. He was conscious of the danger but was distressed that he had not realized the threat was not imminent but was upon them already. He tried to hide his fears from Sophia and Mariah.

Cautiously he said, "Mariah, you have a slight tremor in your speech, which that tells me you are very frightened. This worries me, as I don't want panic to overcome your reasoning. Let's gas up both vehicles and get some coffee and food to eat on our way out of town." Slowly Eli released Mariah from his grip. He gave her a big kiss, stepped back, and said, "Right behind me, OK?"

Eli began his trip, thinking about everything that had taken place. He realized that whoever was after him and his family was obviously positioned to take action. "They're very well organized," Eli said to himself.

He was troubled about what Mariah had encountered at the airport. Again he thought about how well organized they were and how well informed to take whatever action might be necessary to complete their assignment. Like Mariah, he too was curious as to who knew they were going to New York for a funeral and how they had learned that information. The events at the airport added credibility to the rabbi's warning.

After several hours on the highway and passing through small mountain towns, Eli decided to stop and gas up the cars, stretch his legs, and see if the women wanted anything to eat or drink. He wanted to learn more about what had happened at the airport.

Eli put on his turn signal and pulled off the highway onto an exit ramp. He followed the road for a short distance and pulled into the gas station parking lot. Mariah and Sophia were right behind him.

After topping off both cars with gas, they went into the shop for coffee. As they entered the store, they chose a table and were met by a waitress with a welcoming smile.

The waitress came to their table to take their order. "Three coffees please," said Eli.

After the coffee had arrived, Eli noticed Mariah staring straight ahead at something. "What's up? What are you staring at?"

Mariah responded, "Eli, that man has a paper in his hand, but he hasn't turned a page since we came in. I think he's been watching us in our reflection in the window from the time we came in. He's dressed in the same dark clothing as the men at the airport."

Eli was uneasy but remained silent. Sophia was becoming just as anxious as her mother, and Eli could feel the fear radiating from both of them. "Mariah, maybe you're letting your imagination work overtime. He was here before we pulled in, so he wasn't following us."

Mariah was thinking about Eli's last comment as she continued to watch the man. "Maybe," Mariah began to say, "they know about the cabin and they have men all along the various routes watching for us." Mariah's hand shook, causing her cup to clatter while she tried to make a connection with the saucer.

The man stood up and placed his bill with money on the table. Mariah's anxiety rose as he turned and was now facing her direction. There was a pause before he started walking toward their table. He looked at Mariah, and then the man began to place his hat on his head. When he reached their table, he tipped his hat, saying, "Evening, ladies," and continued to walk out the door into the parking lot.

Eli watched as the man opened his car door and took his place behind the driver's seat. Slowly the car pulled out of the lot and exited back onto the highway. The man's car pulled over to the edge of the road. Eli said, "We will wait for a moment, and then we will go."

No one was speaking at the table. Each was keeping an eye on the car and its driver. Finally Eli said, "We need to go. Remember, keep very close to me." Eli walked to his car, and Sophia and Mariah walked to Sophia's car. Eli led the way back onto the highway. He noticed in his rearview mirror that Mariah and Sophia were right behind him. As Eli passed the parked car, he noticed the driver had a small light illuminating a map he was reading.

Eli kept a watchful eye as they continued to travel deeper into the mountains. Checking his rearview mirror frequently, Eli made sure Mariah remained just behind him.

Eli was thinking about what Mariah had said at the café and was beginning to wonder if there was any possibility that people were already there searching for them. *Perhaps*, he thought, *the one knew about the rabbi's cabin.*

After a few hours, they arrived at the cabin. The cabin was up on a hillside, secluded from view with the aid of numerous tall pines. Eli parked his car in the garage, and Mariah followed, parking Sophia's car beside Eli's.

Eli walked to the front door of the cabin and used the key the rabbi had given him. He wanted to make sure they had the right cabin and that the key worked. Mariah and Sophia were right beside him.

After successfully opening the front door, Eli walked into the charming little cabin. Before him was a small living room that was furnished with a couch, two chairs, a coffee table, and three lamps. There was a wood-burning fireplace with dry firewood placed neatly on a wire rack in the corner. Directly beyond the living room was the kitchen with a table with chairs. Dividing the kitchen from the living room was a breakfast bar with barstools.

Stepping further into the cabin, Eli saw a doorway to his left that opened into a hallway. He said, "I am closing the front door and locking it. Please do not use this door as I don't want to take a chance on being seen. I'll use the garage door entrance, which appears to be just off the kitchen, to get our suitcases, and I am also closing the garage door so nobody can tell someone is here."

Mariah and Sophia walked into the kitchen and looked through the cabinets. The kitchen was furnished with cooking and eating necessities to accommodate six people. However, only spices were in the cupboard in addition to coffee, powdered cream, and sugar. Mariah was glad she had brought groceries.

Sophia walked down the short hallway, exploring the rest of the cabin. Mentally she noted the cabin's layout. Taking a few steps forward, she opened the door in front of her. It was a Jack and Jill bathroom. She chuckled a little. "Mom," she called out, "I found the bathroom and laundry room, and I am certain that two bedrooms are at either side of this bathroom door."

Opening the bathroom door located on the left, Sophia entered a room containing a bed, a dresser, a small hope chest at the foot of the bed, a closet, and a window. The bed was made. The numerous pillows gave an alluring appeal to the eye. Sophia was tempted to plop herself among the pillows and get some sleep. She walked to the window, which opened toward the front section of the cabin, to see the surrounding area, but the view was blocked by pine trees.

Walking swiftly back through the bathroom, Sophia opened the other door. She beheld another bedroom decorated very similarly to the other. This room's window provided a view of the back area of the cabin. A trail from the backyard went downward toward a gully.

Eli returned from the car with suitcases. Mariah advised him to find Sophia and see which bedroom she had chosen. Eli walked down the hall and heard Sophia in the room to his right. He turned to the left and placed his and Mariah's suitcases near the dresser.

He looked around in amazement at the room's décor. It was perfect, and the bed looked very inviting. Eli turned to go back to the car and get the rest of the luggage when Sophia and Mariah could be heard in the other room.

Eli went to see what they were so giggly about. Just as Eli was arriving, he heard Sophia say, "You've got to see the other room, Mother. It is spectacular. Whoever decorated these rooms was a master at comfort and simplicity." The women were delighted with the room's arrangement and colors.

Both women exited the room, excusing themselves as they brushed by Eli and continued down the hall to see the other bedroom. He was glad to hear the small talk and to see them happy.

While they were chatting about the décor, Eli went back to the car and brought in the last of the suitcases. He placed Sophia's suitcase and other items she brought in the room to the right of the hallway. Eli looked out the window and saw a path heading down into a gully.

Mariah and Sophia met Eli in the hall and commented on the wonderful cabin they had as a sanctuary from the world. Eli peeked quickly into the room he and Mariah would be sharing. He looked out the window and noticed that the view was blocked by a grove of pine trees. Eli left the bedroom and went into the living room.

All three entered the kitchen area and began helping to prepare their meal; Mariah and Sophia were putting the main dish and vegetables together while discussing various aspects of their situation. The crate and its significance needed to be researched. The robe seemed like it would be an interesting item to investigate. Eli said, "Shouldn't we start with the letters first? They may contain information and give us directions as to where to go."

Eli, while making the coffee, discussed what he would miss about the rabbi. He explained how mesmerizing the rabbi was when explaining stories from the Bible. "I felt like I was right there within the history he was presenting."

Eli paused for a moment and began to speak in a more-serious tone. "I just remembered that I have not told you everything concerning Addison's call. Addison called to inform us that Patrick was not only strange but also that the ledger that was in Patrick's sole possession—actually Edward's ledger—had been altered. Addison said the writing was similar to Patrick's handwriting but done in a wild manner. Addison also said Patrick was trying very hard to get details from Addison about the dig in Alexandria. Addison is in the process of hiding his journal and will try to contact us later with facts that only he and Edward knew. He also hinted that he has data and items that he felt we need to utilize now."

"Addison is really smart, and I think he will be invaluable in deciphering these letters from the rabbi," interjected Sophia.

Mariah asked, "Why do you think Addison would be better than us at deciphering the letters from the rabbi?"

"I don't know," replied Sophia, "But I have a feeling Addison knows more than we think he knows about the crate and the robe, and our finding hidden clues may trigger a knowledge he has but did not realize was important."

"Addison does not have my cell phone number," said Eli. "I need to call him because he said he was heading to a place of safety, and he will tell us how to get to where he is when we speak. However, he must know how to contact us first if we are to meet and discuss the situation."

Everyone was quiet for several moments. Sophia advised her parents that she had completed some of what she considered important research while en route to the cabin.

"I did find that the rabbi died of a heart attack just outside the synagogue. Mom, you may have been the last person he spoke to before he went to the synagogue. The local newspaper stated that a man paused for a moment beside the rabbi, as if giving a prayer over him, and disappeared as soon as the paramedics arrived.

"I am at a loss about the crate Edward was interested in, as most of the information about Edward's digs no longer exists. I researched the missing pieces from the time Edward was in charge at the Alexandria dig; Edward's missing pieces seem to be unremarkable storage containers."

"Why would Edward's research be removed from the database?" Eli remarked. "You have to have financial backing and permission from the places where you are conducting an archeological dig, and everyone involved requires a lot of documentation, much of which is kept in the database."

"Tell your father what you learned about deliveries to the docks," Mariah said to Sophia.

"I checked the charts of incoming crates to the museum on the day Shamar went to pick up your crate," Sophia responded, looking at her father. "I discovered that two crates were delivered on the same day; one was for Patrick, and the other was for you. Each came from New York, but Patrick's was from a different part of New York. I believe Patrick has your crate and the one sent to him could still be sitting on a shelf at the museum dock."

"Enough on the missing crate," Eli remarked. "I think it is time that we examine the box we do have—the red one that the rabbi sent to you with the robe in it."

Mariah retrieved the red box, and they opened it again, but this time they went over the robe in detail. They were surprised to see that the silver-and-gold-embroidered snake had the head of a dragon.

"This is interesting," said Sophia. "Dragons, in some cultures, give out a radiant or magnificent spiritual aura that is perceived as helping mankind when the need arises. I've also read that a snake with a dragon's head partners with Draco; this snake/dragon is a female who is the ever-present companion of Draco. Both are considered fierce protectors of mankind, because the constellation never sets."

Mariah's curiosity was piqued about the dragon and snake. Eli was dumbfounded with Sophia's information about snakes and dragons. He could not remember hearing of this philosophy.

Mariah held the robe close to her chest so everyone could view the snake with the dragon's head. She shivered as she felt coldness pass through her. Within seconds of the shiver, she commented, "Someone must have just walked on my grave, as a cold chill has passed through me. Does anyone else feel this coldness? And what's that whistling sound? What an odd noise—it sounds kind of creepy."

Eli and Sophia noticed that Mariah had become stationary, and her face was turning pale. "What's wrong, Mariah?" Eli yelled. He grabbed Mariah, placing his arms around her in a protective manner.

All three of them heard the thud of an object dropping on the living room floor very close to Mariah. Eli and Sophia glanced up at the ceiling, expecting to see damage.

The ceiling was still intact. Everyone was shocked to see Shamar and someone else lying limp on the floor, close to where Mariah stood.

They were stunned and speechless.

Mariah appeared to be shaken up, so Eli quickly directed her away from the two individuals lying on the floor. Sophia hurried to Shamar's side while Eli checked on the other individual. "Shamar, Shamar, it's me, Sophia? Can you hear me? Shamar you have to be OK!"

Eli confirmed out loud that both men were alive but unconscious and very cold. Their clothes were damp with a layer of frost. Eli remembered telling Mariah how silly she was to always pack her electric blankets, but now he knew they would come in handy. He rushed to the bedroom to get sheets and blankets. Returning to the living room, Eli called out to Mariah, "Remove the men's clothing now, and Sophia start warming sheets, blankets, and robes in the dryer."

Eli and Mariah removed the moist clothing, tossing them toward the laundry closet, where Sophia stood. Eli hollered to Sophia, "Please wash their clothing so when they come around they will have something warm and dry to wear."

Eli removed the pouch from older man's waist and felt a hesitation pass through him. Redirecting his thoughts, he tossed the pouch onto the coffee table. For some reason, Eli did not want the pouch far away from him. Instead he wanted to ensure it was protected. Eli looked to Mariah and said, "I want to see what is in this pouch before we clean it."

Mariah had finished taking all the wet clothes off Shamar and wrapped him in a sheet and blankets. She placed the electric blanket's setting on low. Eli completed undressing the older man and remarked, "He is so cold, Mariah, and I am worried he might not survive. A man of his age should not be exposed to such extreme temperatures; it could induce a heart attack. I hope he makes it; I hope they both make it."

Eli finished wrapping the older man and covered him with an electric blanket, set it on low, and then began to stoke the fire for extra heat.

Sophia brought some warmed sheets to her parents to place over the men. She stated, "They aren't real warm but should do. I thought too much warmth might hurt."

Eli opened the pouch he found on the older man's body and poured its contents upon the coffee table. He found a small scroll case, an unusual scroll that had been folded carefully, and keys. Turning to Sophia, Eli threw the damp pouch toward her and requested it also be cleaned too.

"Now we wait," Eli said out loud.

Sophia joined her parents on the couch. Sophia asked, "How did they get here? What on earth could have frozen them, and who is the stranger? From the way they landed, it is obvious that Shamar was protecting the old man, but from what or who?"

Eli, in a solemn voice, expressed his concerns. "We must wait for them to answer those questions, along with many others. I am sure we will have many, but for now let's concentrate on keeping them warm and as comfortable as possible." Still curious about how the men had gotten there, he ran to the various windows to see if there was a vehicle. There was none. Something had to bring them; people don't just appear out of thin air.

Mariah, in silence, gently folded her red robe and placed it back into the red box. Eli asked her to wait a moment, as he wanted to look closer at the snake. Everyone focused on the robe as Mariah held it up again. It was an elegantly embroidered silver and gold snake with a dragon's head.

Eli turned his attention to the items he had tossed upon the coffee table. It seemed to be an odd assortment of strange-looking silver coins and a miniature scroll case. The coins looked like replicas of ancient Roman currency.

Picking up the miniature case, Eli felt a twinge of shame fall over him, so he placed the case back down. It could wait.

His mind wandered as he tried to figure out who the older gentleman might be, how and why Shamar had brought this elderly man with him, and why they had landed there. And how! Thinking for a moment, Eli speculated that the snake robe might have acted as a beacon in conjunction with Shamar's robe.

All of his inquiries would have to wait for answers. For now, Eli's task was keeping the men warm and comfortable.

CHAPTER NINE
Addison Seeks Safety in the Bunker.

Addison could hear Patrick as he entered through the front door. He closed the journal and waited for Patrick to address him. Soon he would know whether Patrick had been successful in his attempt to begin bridging his relationships with the Daniels.

Within moments Patrick called for Addison. Addison knew by the sound of Patrick's voice that he was not successful with his attempt to right many years of a neglected relationship.

Addison began walking from the kitchen toward the front door, answering Patrick's call as he proceeded. "Yes sir, how may I help you?" Patrick's face showed agitation, and for once he said nothing. He just looked to Addison like a lost child seeking help.

"Addison," began Patrick, "I went to the Daniels' house, and Eli wouldn't even let me in the front door. He said that my timing was poor and that he had to go. I feel so miserable because I really need the Daniels' expertise, and I now I think they might never help me. I went to every hospital searching for Shamar, and no information could be given to me. So I drove around thinking about all that has happened, and I realize I have really screwed up."

Addison paused, waiting for Patrick to reach him, "Please come with me to the kitchen. We will have some tea, and I will share my information. I also need you to answer some of my questions." Patrick became cautious and silent as he walked beside Addison toward the kitchen.

Addison stepped slightly in front of Patrick to open the kitchen door. Addison asked Patrick to please have a seat, pointing to the table. It seemed to

Patrick as though time were moving very slowly as he sat at the table, waiting for Addison to complete the preparation and pouring of tea.

Sitting down across from Patrick, Addison said, "I have gone over your father's journal, which has been in your possession since his death." Addison paused briefly, sipping tea and watching Patrick's reaction. He continued, "I have compared Edward's journal with my personal notes and have written down the differences here on this sheet of paper."

Addison handed Patrick the sheet of paper and continued. "The wording from your father's journal is in blue ink, and the words from my notes are in black ink."

Addison paused again, allowing Patrick time to examine the notes and come clean about what he knew and what he was up to. Patrick studied the comparison while Addison continued to sip his tea.

After a few moments, Addison placed the teacup into the saucer and expressed his concerns to Patrick. "It appears that particular information is absent from your father's journal. I remember that ninety percent of your father's journal entries involved the Alexandria expedition.

"What amazes me is that someone found the exact crate that your father spent most of his career looking for, and they contacted you and sent the item to you, oddly enough, not to your home but to the museum."

Patrick winced.

"How did that person know where to find the crate and what the crate looked like? How could they know this, Patrick? Who told you they found the crate, and when and where did they find it? What information did they use as research to find the crate, and did that person ever work for your father? I know you did not find the crate from the information in your father's journal because that information is grossly incorrect. Tell me, Patrick, how was this feat accomplished?"

Patrick was fuming inside but kept very quiet and stared down at the note that compared the two journals.

Addison knew from Patrick's silence that he would not get an answer, so he continued. "Now tell me what happened when you went to the Daniels home, and if you are sincere, I would like to help you in your effort to put your life back together."

Patrick began to explain to Addison, "Well, Mr. Daniels answered the front door and told me my timing was bad. I apologized for the incident at the docks and said I needed Sophia's help in finding the answers that my father could not find on his last quest. Eli refused to listen. He closed the front door and locked it. I turned around and left."

Addison commented, "That is not good, Patrick, but please continue."

Patrick remained silent, studying his tea.

Addison went on, "The people who assisted your father while in Alexandria, Egypt, are all dead except for me, Eli, and Mariah. I wonder now whether the person who had them eliminated will also come after me too."

Leaning forward in his chair and looking straight into Patrick's face, Addison in a firm voice said, "Yes I did say eliminated because each person I researched died under unusual circumstances—every single one of them.

"Most died from heart attacks. Your father, however, died from a disease of the lungs. I checked into his affliction and discovered it usually is contracted from contaminated mummies. Your father, Eli, Mariah, and I never worked near mummies at our sites. So I've always wondered how he got this disease.

"It seems to me that if one person contracts a particular disease, especially from a contaminated area, that others also present at that site should be infected too. Rarely is just one person inflicted with a communicable disease in which many workers were present. That being said, your father died from a disease he could only have contracted by working with mummies, and no one else caught it "Your father knew this day could come, and that drastic preparations would be needed and in place to protect you, and at the time he also wanted to keep your mother from harm. However, I don't think that we can hide for very long from the individual who is seeking information about the dig and the items we found there.

"I suspect Sago Kragulijac. He's a deranged man, power hungry and wealthy enough to be extremely dangerous. This individual has the ability, knowledge, and money to achieve whatever he wants. Also he's smart enough to understand that my demise and that of anyone else associated with your father and his dig in Alexandria must look like accidents. Patrick, do you realize that your life and mine are in danger?"

Patrick was stunned and momentarily speechless. Slowly he sat up very stiff and erect in his chair, as if at attention, before responding to Addison. "Who's Sago, how do you know him, and why do you suspect him? And what on earth could be so important that someone would go to these lengths to kill my father and maybe you too for trinkets from an archeological dig?"

Addison responded to Patrick while offering him another cup of tea, "Sago is someone I've encountered in the past who has been responsible for some unfortunate events."

Patrick moved his cup and saucer toward Addison and stared at him as Addison filled his tea cup. The anxiety on Patrick's face exposed fright and concern. In silence they drank their tea.

When Patrick and Addison finished their tea they straightened up in the kitchen. Addison washed the dishes and Patrick put everything away. Addison wiped down the kitchen table and placed the doily and flowers at the table's center.

Patrick's cell phone rang. He glanced at it to see who was calling. "Excuse me," was the last thing Addison heard as Patrick quickly left the kitchen.

Addison went to a small enclave in his kitchen and called Gabriel. Here he felt comfortable knowing that he could whisper into the phone without being overheard.

While the phone was ringing, Addison kept a close watch on the kitchen door. "Gabriel," began Addison, "listen to me carefully, and follow my directions to the letter. I believe your life and mine are in grave danger. I need you to come to Patrick's home, but make sure no one sees you. Meet me in the courtyard by the cascading flowerpots on the wall. Stay hidden. There is much I need to explain to you. It would be preferable if you parked your car a good distance from Patrick's home and make sure it is well hidden. Patrick can't know about our meeting."

Gabriel replied, "I'm very close and can be there in a matter of minutes. Are you OK, Addison?" Addison responded that everything was all right and then ended the call.

Addison left the kitchen and was looking around the house, ensuring that everything was tidy when Patrick bolted from the study. He said to Addison as he was running past him, "Gotta run. See you later."

Addison was only slightly surprised by Patrick's actions. He continued doing his nightly inspection of all the windows and doors, making sure everything was in order. With his final trip to the study, Addison took the crate from the bookcase and departed for the garden, where he pressed a hand control activating a hidden opening. The wall split open, exposing steps leading downward.

Gabriel jumped from behind the moving wall and exclaimed, "Holy cow, Addison!" Addison put his fingers to his lips, informing Gabriel to be quiet. "Follow me," were Addison's next words.

Addison and Gabriel began their descent down the staircase. It was wide, and they could see spiraling stairs that seemed to continue into an endless downward abyss. When Addison reached a certain step of his descent, lights illuminated the remaining stairs.

Both felt the cooler air as they reached a grand opening before them. This room was large. Addison immediately pushed a small switch on the wall and listened as the wall moved back into position, followed by a click and then the sharp sound of a lock snapping into place.

Addison waited for the sound of the sprinklers beginning their function. "Everything should be as it was," Addison said to Gabriel. "The sprinklers will cover any footprints and help in hiding us from intruders.

"Please have a seat," Addison said to Gabriel, gesturing to the large couch before them. Gabriel sat down, contemplating what was going on. He was very surprised that this place existed. Addison understood the surprised look on Gabriel's face and said to him, "I am going to explain this underground bunker to you and why it exists. Then together we must plan our strategy. Our lives are dependent on Eli figuring out my references to the robes and following my verbal instructions to the letter."

***

Eli checked to see if the clothes were dry. Finding they were still damp, he removed the elder man's pouch and reset the dryer for more time.

Carrying the pouch with him to the sofa, Eli returned the elder gentleman's items back to the pouch, still contemplating who this stranger could be.

Eli heard some moaning from the floor and quickly moved toward Shamar. Eli could tell Shamar was beginning to awaken.

In a few moments, Shamar made eye contact with Eli, saying out loud, "Oh my God, it worked! You are here, and we are with you. But where are we?"

Eli replied, "How did you appear out of nowhere, and who is that with you?"

Shamar excitedly answered, "Eli, you won't believe what I've done. I don't believe it myself." Looking around and seeing Theon, Shamar asked, "What happened to my friend, and is he OK?"

Eli answered, "I think so. You and this man have been unconscious since you popped in a few hours ago. How did you get here, seemingly out of nowhere, and who is this man?"

Shamar hesitated before answering. Then he said, "You're not going to believe me, and I still don't believe it myself." Shamar stopped his conversation with Eli because he heard a soft moan from Theon's direction.

Shamar rushed over to Theon, exclaiming, "We made it, Theon. However, we've been unconscious for a few hours. Are you OK?"

Theon replied, "I'm cold."

Shamar said he was cold too. Eli grabbed the pajamas and said, "Here are some clothes for each of you."

Slowly becoming aware of his surroundings, Theon was immediately astonished at the artificial light illuminating the room.

"Theon, this is Eli, who I spoke to you about," Shamar explained, gesturing toward Theon and then to Eli.

Eli said, "Hurry up and finish dressing. The pajamas and the robe will warm you up."

Theon, puzzled by such unfamiliar garments, watched Shamar slip into his. After getting the pajamas on, Theon looked around and commented to Shamar, "We really are in the future."

Shamar said to Eli, "You won't believe me, but I was transported back in time to Alexandria, Egypt, specifically the great Library of Alexandria. Theon is the caretaker of the Library of Alexandria."

Eli, thinking about the strange coins, and acknowledging that Shamar and Theon had appeared out of nowhere onto the living room floor, said out loud, "I'm starting to get the picture. But how did you get there?"

Shamar smiled and said, "The robe, Eli."

Theon noted the confused look on Eli's face and solemnly said, "Eli, I uncovered really frightening and important information about a religious artifact that has been hidden within the Library of Alexandria for centuries.

"I learned that someone else is frantically searching for this artifact. I discovered from my research the reason for seeking the crystal but not *who* is seeking it. I am surprised that none of you are aware of what is at stake, so I chose to share with all of you my knowledge so that together we can combine our facts and secure the artifact before the assassins find us. Yes, there are assassins hired to get this artifact and they have no regard for life."

Eli was still struggling with the idea of time travel. Confused, he asked, "So are these assassins in your time or ours?"

Theon responded, "I don't know, perhaps both. Or perhaps they also travel in time, or maybe their organization has kept up this search through the centuries. It is important that each of you grasp that the individuals hired to seek us out were hired by a deadly secret organization and the loss of some or all of us is unimportant to them. I don't know how we became intertwined, but I believe our lives are in grave danger, and these assassins are just a small step behind us."

The men became aware of approaching footsteps from the other room. They turned in unison to see Mariah and Sophia rushing down the hall way. Sophia hurried over to Shamar and gave him a welcoming embrace with an equally welcoming kiss. Shamar responded in kind.

Mariah waited a moment, and then she gave Shamar a gentle kiss on the cheek and a hug followed by, "Welcome home, Shamar. I have a bone to pick with you. Where have you been? We have been very worried about you—" Eli stopped Mariah and suggested that she listen instead of scolding Shamar.

Eli apologized, quickly introduced the women to Theon, and asked Shamar and Theon to continue. Shamar and Theon, being more alert, began an animated description of events that had happened at the docks and the events in Alexandria. They interrupted each other frequently, with both trying to explain everything at once.

Theon cleared his throat. He shifted into a more serious tone and explained, "What is important here is what Shamar and I have discovered. This is what I know: Alexander the Great, after conquering Persia, helped himself to a unique item from the treasury room, one that has been described as a crystal and a gem. When he wore this item or carried it upon his person into battle, wounds he received that should have been fatal healed quickly, and he returned to good health at an accelerated rate. This is one of the reasons someone seeks this crystal, because of its perceived healing power and the ability to cheat death."

Eli said, "I still do not understand what this has to do with me and my family. There is no such crystal at the museum, and none of us has done an archeological dig for such an item."

Mariah said, "Eli, it could be that when we went to Alexandria to work with Edward, it was thought that we knew something we did not. That gem might be what Edward was searching for without telling us, and now those mysterious seekers think we know something."

Then Sophia burst into the conversation, asking Theon, "Are our lives in danger, and is there anything else you learned about this crystal that we should know? How dangerous are these seekers?"

Theon immediately answered, "Why yes there is. Aristotle was the person at the library who hid Alexander's treasures or contraband. When Aristotle heard of Alexander's death, he assembled the best men from the library to help him in not just hiding specific treasures but making it more or less impossible for others to decipher clues to its hiding place. These clues are literally scattered now due to treasure seekers finding portions of the clues and thinking they had the entire clue.

"The men who created the clues were experts in cryptic communication and had the ability to send messages to one another with clues that were visible yet hidden in the text so that even the courier could not recognize the secret message.

"To ensure that Alexander's generals could not find Alexander's contraband, those men spent weeks formulating the enduring after-death secret. These men spent the rest of their lives carving into a special stick a symbolic mark with each year that passed and Alexander's generals were unsuccessful at finding the treasure. That stick is in the secret room of the library, and I assume the last entry was by the last survivor of the enduring after-death group.

"Yes, Sophia, the persons seeking not only the crystal but any knowledge connected with it were extremely dangerous individuals, even in the years before my time. People were tortured for information, and all who were gathered by the seekers' assassins were killed. I would venture to guess that they are just as dangerous in your time."

Sophia inquisitively looked at Theon and asked, "What kind of coding did they use? Were you able to decode some or the entire enduring after-death secret, and how long have you known this code?"

Eli quickly connected Theon's information about coding and writing notes and shouted, "Wait a minute. I'm certain Theon can assist in decoding the rabbi's letters."

Theon and Shamar stated simultaneously, "What letters?"

As Eli was heading into the living room to get the letters, Mariah answered Theon and Shamar's question. "The rabbi sent letters to Eli over several years, and in his final letter to Eli, the rabbi stated there were hidden clues tucked into the letters.

"We only skimmed the letters since it didn't dawn on us how important they might be. We certainly have not given them the complete attention they need. Theon, could you please help us examine the letters and let us know if you see any clues such as those used by the enduring after-death group?"

Eli placed the matchbox, letters, and fragile scroll from the rabbi in front of Theon. Eli was energized with renewed hope that Theon was the answer to finding the clues the rabbi mentioned.

Eli said to Theon, "Please examine this papyrus that is from the distant past and this letter from the rabbi about his family, and tell me if there is anything in this matchbox that will help. I don't understand the matchbox but believe it is of some, importance since he sent it to me on the same day he died.

"I know you and Shamar are on target when you state our lives are in danger, but we don't know who we are hiding from or why. I will give you more details of our encounters after you have checked the letters from the rabbi. Let us know if you think there is information in these letters that will help us."

Mariah asked, "Does my robe have any bearing on the situation, or is it just Shamar's robe?"

Theon was surprised to hear of another robe. He answered, "Yes, your robe is important too. What robe are you speaking of, and may I see it?"

Mariah left the room for her bedroom to get the robe.

Eli asked, "Do you think the robe that the rabbi sent us is connected with this enduring after-death secret?"

Theon answered, "I can give you my opinion as soon as I see the robe."

"Eli," began Theon, "I am interested in the old parchment because I am still looking for two special scrolls. These scrolls could be any size. Do you know how the rabbi came into possession of the artifact or the robes? I am curious too as to what was in the crate."

Eli responded, "Addison said three flasks were in the crate."

Theon and Shamar each took in deep breaths of astonishment as they heard the mention of three flasks. The shocked look on their faces revealed that something was wrong—terribly wrong.

Theon in a very sheepish voice said, "We are in far greater danger now that the flasks have been exposed to the atmosphere. Shamar and I read that once the flasks are exposed to the air, the flasks send a beacon into the atmosphere alerting good and evil that they are ready to yield their information. This increases the lethal probability as we move forward. How long ago did he expose the flasks to the air?"

Eli said, "I would guess sometime in the last fifteen to twenty hours. You did say good and evil, so wouldn't there be more assistance for us, the good side, of course?"

Shamar replied, "We are the good side, Eli. I doubt there are others who have the knowledge of the after-death secret, and if they did, they would not want to participate in such a deadly exploration. The odds of success are dim because of what and who we stand up against."

Sophia said, "I'm scared, but I choose to help Shamar and Theon with this battle. I will use my knowledge to help them."

Eli was quick to answer. "Don't volunteer yourself, Sophia. This is a dangerous path that needs to be pursued by Theon, Shamar, and me. I want you and your mother to remain here."

Mariah returned with the red robe. An eerie silence filled the room, and Mariah knew something was said in her absence. Without a word, Mariah offered the robe to Theon.

Theon began to examine it, and he noticed as he unfolded it that the craftsmanship was just as magnificent as Shamar's robe. Everyone was also taking in the robe and its unique embroidery threads with detailed stitching and glistening crystals adding to the snake's detail.

Mariah asked what had happened while she was gone. Eli and Sophia both began to answer her question. Sophia successfully spoke over her father. "We

The Thirteenth Stone of Aaron

learned that the flasks Addison spoke to Father about are now more dangerous to us. It seems that when the flasks were exposed to air, each flask sent out a beacon to both good and evil of their presence. Evil wants the knowledge that each flask holds to assist them in their desire, and good wants it to overcome the evil."

Mariah's jaw dropped visibly, and she said, "What have you decided to do, Eli?"

"I am going to help Theon and Shamar finish this task," Eli replied. "I want you and Sophia to stay here."

Everyone could see Mariah as she seemed to come unglued with Eli's response. "We will not stay here. Sophia and I have abilities to assist with the task, and we will each help wherever Theon thinks we are needed."

Theon sat back in his chair, watching all that was taking place. Calmly he said, "This is just what evil would like, for each of us to argue among ourselves and waste time deciding who will do what. Perhaps we should open the papyrus and matchbox, as I believe we were meant to discuss their contents together so we can take the appropriate actions together. May I have a look at the papyrus and matchbox contents please?"

Eli pushed the papyrus, matchbox, and scraps of paper directly in front of Theon. Theon asked for paper and pen. When Eli supplied these items, Theon paused and looked confused. "Where is the inkwell?" Everyone smiled, and Shamar explained to Theon that the pen had a shaft full of ink and therefore he did not need an inkwell.

Theon began to examine the matchbox first. Mariah and Sophia took a seat, one on each side of Theon, so they could observe his examination of the items. Shamar sat directly across from Theon, prepared to take notes if needed. Opening the tiny matchbox, Theon found the missing traveling prayers. They had been folded precisely to fit where they had been placed. This discovery surprised Theon.

Eli handed Theon a small old key, stating that it had also fit perfectly into the matchbox, secured within the small scroll pieces. The rabbi had sent it separately, with no instructions. Theon thanked Eli. He looked at the key, gently wrapped it in the traveling scrolls, and placed them back into the matchbox.

Handing the matchbox back to Eli, Theon said, "We desperately need the contents of this matchbox back at the library, Eli. The contents are significantly important to the task at hand. Please guard the box well, and always carry it with you."

Theon began to examine the papyrus. Slowly, he sketched his own interpretation from the symbols he saw veiled within the papyrus. Sophia and Mariah were mesmerized while watching him draw on the paper.

Mariah thought to herself, *who would guess that these symbols were pictorial words?* She remarked out loud, "What else have I missed at archaeological sites that was before me and yet hidden in symbols?"

Sophia stared at the ancient papyrus and back at Theon's drawings; gently, she grasped both pieces of paper and spent several minutes comparing the separate images and Theon's interpretation. She was amazed at the intellect that had been employed so many centuries ago. Her mind was racing with awe and a new respect at how simple wording was intertwined with pictorial information.

Theon was fascinated by Sophia's comprehensive skill with words and pictures. He wanted to take her to the secret room to introduce her to the reams of documents there. Perhaps later.

Theon, assembling the information, finally said, "I have some valuable information to share with all of you, but first let me say this rabbi was a very wise and intelligent man who desired to gather all the essential items required to stop evil before it consumed humanity. He hid information right within the sight of those who read but did not see what was written. So here is the first of two messages that I deciphered.

"This message refers to ancient gods and their seven gates to the supplementary world where old ones, the gods of evil, often referred to in our Judeo-Christian world as the devil, wait for the perfect time when they can return victoriously to rule the world. The opening of the crate reawakened the evil gods' desire for powers held in the flasks. They now seek to destroy a crystal that restrains the full potential of their powers, and the flasks that support the sacred crystal. They will send their minions to seek and destroy all associated with the releasing of the powers from the flasks."

The room was still. Everyone was speechless. Eli, amazed at the information Theon had managed to extract, said, "We need to contact Addison immediately. His life hangs in the balance."

Mariah, after recovering from her amazement at his cleverness, let loose a barrage of questions. "What is the other message? Are we in danger if we use the robes? Are you confident that wearing the robes will not harm us? Do these robes place us in danger? Will these robes protect us from evil or just lead us into a confrontation?"

Theon responded, "First, the other message is a reference to a secret tunnel back in Alexandria. About the robes—these robes are of great significance, and the rabbi did not send them to you to speculate about their abilities but to use them. He sacrificed his life to get these items to you, Eli.

"We must each entrust our diverse capabilities and combined knowledge to help each other to move forward to complete this mission. The rabbi chose wisely when he decided on you. Mariah and Sophia bring the strength of knowledge about cultures from the past, along with languages and cultures.

"Shamar brings the strength of courage and willingness to choose good over evil. And you, Eli, bring a different strength that will unite us, and that is your gift of protection to family, friends, and a united cause. I know you will protect all of us. We need the skills and abilities found within each of to be successful in this undertaking."

Shamar said, "I suggest that we get to Addison as quickly as possible. Since we do not know about the red robe, I propose we leave it here at the cabin. Using my robe, we can hold on to each other to travel. Eli, you hold on to Mariah, Sophia will hold on to me, and Theon will be in the middle, holding onto whoever he chooses. We will keep him protected in the middle."

"Wait a minute," said Eli. "If we are traveling to where Addison is, how do we know the robe will get us there? And if we are traveling anywhere, I want to take the backpack with the letter from the rabbi and the matchbox too."

Shamar and Theon changed back into their clothes. Mariah grabbed the red robe and hung it in the front room closet.

Before everyone gathered, Sophia spoke to Shamar in the hall. "Shamar, I'm scared. When this first started happening, I thought my father was overreacting, but now I'm frightened, really frightened."

Shamar embraced Sophia and said, "I will always be here for you, Sophia. When I was in Alexandria, I thought about you and me, and I just couldn't imagine my life without you. I love you, and I will do my best to protect you."

Sophia smiled and gave Shamar a bigger hug and kiss. "I love you too, Shamar."

Eli spoke to Mariah and said he hadn't realized the trouble they were in, and now he thought describing it as cloak and dagger was an understatement.

Everyone gathered together. Eli asked again, "How do we know the robe will take us to Addison? And shouldn't we take some warm clothes? Apparently this method of travel dissipates much of our body heat."

Shamar reminded them about the rabbi's instruction not to let the robe be adjacent to artificial fibers. "Perhaps we should dress only in cotton and wool and bring along some coats and bathrobes."

After preparing as much as they could, they gathered together and looked at Theon.

Theon said, "We must have confidence in those watching over us." He pulled a prayer from his pouch and began to read it. The process was slow at first, and then everyone began to spin simultaneously. The spinning increased, the atmosphere began to chill to a bitter cold, and all light faded away.

CHAPTER TEN
Crisis in the Bunker.

Addison and Gabriel walked slowly around the bunker, with Addison explaining each room to Gabriel. Addison remarked that he did not want this to be their tomb. Addison explained how well Edward had planned each detail and had taken such care in choosing the appropriate supplies to support a long underground stay. There was a kitchen, a study, four bedrooms, a large dining area, a three-tier storage room, a living room, and a water storage area.

Generous double doors were located on either side of the entrance to the kitchen. The double doors to the left of the kitchen entrance led to an enormous water-containment area. The double doors to the right of the kitchen area opened to a wide walk-in food storage area, which was layered into three sections. The first segment had steps leading down into the second subdivision, and the second section had steps leading down into the final area. Each section was full of food, utensils, and paper supplies. Enough food and supplies were within this area to last many years. The first floor also contained foot lockers.

Upon returning to the kitchen, Addison asked Gabriel to help him to move a certain section of the wall sideways. He did, and to his surprise, he saw a hidden room.

Addison stepped forward and drew Gabriel's attention to a glass showcase with a few items displayed within it. The wall in front of him had a large map of ancient Alexandria that was encased between two layers of glass. Addison turned to Gabriel and said, "These are items that Edward found on one his digs. I have taken care of them since his death."

Bringing his attention back to the glass case, Addison observed three small jars, a robe, and a few small crystals displayed within an opened sea shell. Addison asked Gabriel to go back to the entrance and bring the crate he had placed on the floor. When Gabriel returned with the crate, Addison asked him to place it in the upper corner of the glass case. He did.

Addison and Gabriel were leaving the room when they heard a faint whistling noise. Addison pivoted around, looking for the noise's origin. Gabriel asked, "What is that, Addison?"

Addison looked down at his watch. The feeling of dread ran through Addison as his heart began to pound; he thought that perhaps the evil entity within Patrick or worse had found them.

The whistling sound grew stronger, and a cold breeze began to travel through the room. Soon a loud thump accompanied by the sound of shrieks could be heard. The room became silent, and Addison and Gabriel saw before them Eli, Mariah, Sophia, Shamar, and an old man dressed oddly.

Unlike the other transportations, it only took a moment for the travelers to acquaint themselves with their surroundings. Eli smiled at Addison and moved to him, giving him a big hug.

"You're late," said Addison

Mariah said, "Where are we?"

Sophia remarked, "Oh my gosh, look—another robe."

Theon and Shamar were studying their surroundings. Shamar noticed Gabriel and spoke up forcibly, "You! What are you doing here? This is the man from the docks who had his men beat me."

Shamar rushed to Gabriel, grabbed him, and began a fistfight. Both men rolled on the floor into the kitchen, punching each other in the process. Shamar had the upper hand and swung at Gabriel's face. Gabriel blocked his punch and yelled to Shamar, "I don't want to hurt you. I'm sorry for what happened at the docks. It is because of the hurt I caused the Daniels that I have quit working for Patrick."

Addison, Theon, and Eli hurried toward both of the men, with Eli grabbing Shamar and Theon helping Gabriel to his feet. The women walked slowly into the kitchen and waited for the explanations to begin.

Addison advised everyone that Gabriel no longer worked for Patrick. He realized that the work Patrick had him do was wrong, and he chose not to engage in any further questionable activities.

After a brief silence, Addison commented on the robe Shamar was wearing. Then Theon said, "I saw another robe in the glass area, and I would like to examine it."

Theon introduced himself to Addison and extended his hand in friendship. Theon felt warmth from Addison as he gave Addison a hardy handshake.

Looking around, Addison responded to the questioning expressions on their faces. "Please, everyone, accompany me to the dining room, and I shall explain many things to you."

Addison showed everyone to the dining room and excused himself for a moment. Everyone seated themselves around the table. Theon chose to sit beside Gabriel.

Addison returned with the robe, a crate, and a leather backpack. Theon stood up and held out his hands for the robe. Addison placed everything on the table, handing Theon the robe.

Addison said, "You have arrived at Edward's bunker. And I am so glad to see each of you."

Shamar stood and introduced Theon to Addison. He stated that Theon was from ancient Alexandria, which seemed not to surprise him. Theon looked in awe at Addison, and for a moment, there seemed to be an understanding or bond between the two men.

Theon stood to answer the question. "We have arrived here with the use of Shamar's robe. I see from the items displayed in the glass case why fate brought us here. Addison, we are in desperate need of the items in the display case, and I feel we should include you in our mission."

Addison jumped into the conversation. "Please allow me to explain something to all of you. Edward had this bunker built as a safe haven for his family. The items in the glass case were brought from Alexandria when Edward and I last visited it.

"Let me back up a little to explain why I am in charge of these items. After objects began to disappear from the dig, Edward thought it necessary to place special items in his private footlocker for safekeeping. When we returned from Egypt, Edward was going to give these things to the museum, but the board was quick to censure him and the thought occurred to Edward that the board would misinterpret his desire to protect the objects in the manner he did but instead assume that he stole them for self-interest."

"So Edward brought contraband from the dig site," Eli said, "and never told anyone about it? How could he do that, Addison? I have vouched for Edward for many years, and now I learn that I defended a thief."

"Edward was not a thief," Addison snapped back at him.

Eli went on, "If Edward had told me the truth, I would have found a way to return the items without any further reflection on his character."

Theon said, "We need to get on with this in a hurry because the door has widened for the minions to come find us. Please, Addison, get to the point, and make it as short and quick as possible."

Addison continued at a faster pace. "Edward's colleague had discovered through personal research that the items he brought back had a value to certain ruthless individuals who were anxious to gather those items as well as any supporting information that accompanied them.

"Edward, out of fear, built this bunker because he knew that in time the someone would figure out that he had the items they so desperately wanted and would come looking for them. It was Rabbi Katz who first approached Edward about the crate…"

"Rabbi Katz," said numerous people simultaneously.

"Yes" replied Addison. "Edward was desperately trying to help the rabbi. Edward wanted to be involved in protecting mankind from evil. Edward was convinced that if the evil ones found these items Rabbi Katz was searching for, the world would change dramatically. And the rabbi's funding for Edward's research was substantial.

"Patrick never knew about Rabbi Katz; only I did. My knowledge of the rabbi was presented to me by Edward to be kept secret, and until this very moment, I have honored that request.

"Anyway, I recognize the robe Shamar is wearing and know that all the robes work in conjunction with the robe Edward brought back from Alexandria."

"So this is why people are after us," Mariah interjected, "because we helped Edward in Alexandria, and they think we know or have items they are searching for."

Addison continued, "I have a sneaking suspicion that Sago Kragulijac is the scoundrel seeking the information and the artifacts Edward hid many years ago. I have kept secret the correspondence from the rabbi and his knowledge of what he and Edward had uncovered. But I believe this is the time to give this paperwork to you so you can use its information to assist you."

Several people began to speak at once, and Eli, wanting to hold back the chatter to a more-organized situation, produced a loud whistle. The room became silent. Speaking up, Eli said, "Let's all put our information in my leather bag for safekeeping. Addison, please give me the communication between Edward and the rabbi. I am of the opinion that we are past the grace period for formulating a plan and must start taking action immediately. Much precious time has passed, and we have made no progress."

Addison said, "Patrick's men did not get the correct crate; they intercepted the crate intended for Eli. I believe that when Sago finds out the crate he was searching for was not the one presented to him, he will be very displeased. Here are the jars, robe, crystals, and two crates. I have the crate Patrick was presented with today and the crate Edward placed his crystal flask into."

"His crystal flask?" interjected Shamar.

"Yes," replied Addison, "Edward's crystal flask. I have never opened the well-wrapped flask and do not know what it looks like. However I have placed it in my leather backpack for traveling."

Eli and Mariah were dazed at the information revealed by Addison. Theon remained silent but was aware of what Addison was describing and now understood which scrolls and symbols would be useful to them.

Everyone was now aware of how extensive the rabbi's involvement was; he had provided funding for the work and had given explicit instructions. It was fascinating to listen as Addison explained various circumstances and aspirations of both the rabbi and Edward concerning artifacts and religious relics.

Addison scooted the backpack in front of him, securing all the straps ensuring its safety for the trip. "As stated earlier, I am certain this crystal flask was designed in Thebes. Not only is the craftsmanship superb, but the technique of crystalline art is masterful."

Shamar and Theon said together, "Thebes?"

Addison answered, "Yes, Thebes. My guess is that each flask's design complements its corresponding robe. Edward found the ceramic pottery that the rabbi anxiously sought, but the rabbi was afraid to come see it or speak of it with Edward."

Looking directly to Theon, Addison asked, "Theon, should I commence with the clay pots first and then the flask or the knowledge about the crystals? I yield to your best judgment."

Theon was considering his response as he slowly stood. "I have listened and observed and am aware of potential circumstances each of us must be prepared for if we are to be successful. Our danger lever has increased substantially. Each flask is now a beacon betraying its whereabouts. If we carry these with us, we take the risk with us too. We cannot turn the communication signal off, so there is no place to hide them either."

There was a long, silent pause before Theon continued. Theon wanted to stress the danger, and his pause was to help build a fire under their desire to complete this quest. "Eli, I believe you are to wear the third robe; please put it on. Addison, I believe you should be the caretaker of the clay pots, the crate, and the crystals. Please place all these items in your traveling bag and bring it with you"—Theon gestured toward the leather backpack—"and secure it tightly to you.

"It is time to travel back to where we must gather information and complete our research and task. That place is ancient Alexandria, specifically the secret room. We must shelter ourselves from the evil now closing in on the beacon's signal. The clay pots I believe were those used by Alexander and his mother to communicate with each other. I will need to work with Sophia at the library to understand the intended meaning of the pictures on the outside of each pot.

"For us to move forward and to be successful, we must complete certain tasks and research the significance of what we are trying to defeat. I would like Shamar to research where the second secret room might be and Eli and Mariah to research where we might look for the scroll of knowledge or secrets and a scroll of fate. Sophia, you are excellent in languages, and I believe you will be needed to decipher what is probably coded information, so I need you to help me in researching how we are to eliminate this evil so this quest can be completed. Each of us must be aware of our enemies' strengths and weaknesses.

"As for the robes, each displays an image that indicates the strength of the wearer. The dragon represents strength and control, and the snake represents the constant watch over mankind in concert with the dragon. The third robe is the robe of communication through the scrolls of knowledge and fate.

The Thirteenth Stone of Aaron

"We must hurry with our travel plans. I would suggest that we form a circle so we may all travel safely together. There are six of us. Eli, you wear the scroll robe, and please hold on to Addison and Mariah. Shamar, you wear the dragon robe and hold on to Sophia and Gabriel. I will be at the center holding on to whomever I grab first."

Everyone returned to the room with the glass case and gathered in the circle as Theon had suggested, preparing to travel to their necessary destination when, out of nowhere, Patrick called out. They all took in a deep breath of surprise.

Addison said, "Patrick, how did you find this bunker?"

Patrick smiled a mischievous smile back at everyone. He answered Addison in a strange voice. "Remember that plastic bag Gabriel gave me? Well, I deciphered the scraps of information included in the crate from the rabbi. It surprised me that you knew so much about the rabbi, Addison, especially the fact that my father was working for him and not the museum. When were you going to share that information with me? I also had someone research for me any additions to this home. Seems my father had this bunker built, and neither he nor you told me about it. I believe it holds items that belong to my father, and I have come to claim those things."

Theon realized the direct threat to their safety, so he stepped in front of Patrick, blocking his path. Theon slowly, and with a saddened voice, began his assessment. "Patrick, you are possessed by a shadow that sprinkles a baptism of gloom upon you daily, waiting for the opportunity to completely engulf your soul. I know a place where you will be safe from any further assaults on your being, and I know of individuals who can rid you of this foul addendum. I ask you to place your confidence in me and those who are now present so that together we may free you."

Patrick appeared uncomfortable or confused as he shifted his weight from foot to foot and was silent.

Looking into Patrick's face, Theon sensed that a distant being was suppressing itself, calculating the perfect time to strike.

Patrick spoke up in a crackly voice. "I would like you to meet my companion who will not surrender himself or me to any of you. In fact, he is here to help me take the items you possess back to our master."

There was silence for several moments while everyone waited for Theon to respond. He did not. Addison had tears running down his face, and he too remained speechless. Addison knew what Theon had stated about Patrick was accurate.

Mariah and Sophia moved closer to Eli, remaining silent, and each holding one of his hands for comfort and protection. Eli squeezed their hands, acknowledging their concern and sending a signal that he was going to protect them and keep them safe.

Shamar seized this uncomfortable moment, and in an unyielding command, he spoke up quickly and decisively. "Everyone re-form our circle and prepare to travel." Everyone ignored Patrick and resumed their position in preparation for travel to Alexandria.

Theon had just pulled the prayer from his pouch and was beginning to read it when a loud crackling noise resounded throughout the entire bunker, while simultaneously a thick, foul-smelling fog formed around everyone within the circle.

Theon's speech was immediately silenced. Theon looked around and noticed no one could speak or move and that each face illustrated alarm at what was happening. Theon recalled from his readings how this method was used by powerful predators to overtake their prey. He understood that everyone in the presence of this lesser evil would soon become a prisoner.

As the fog dissipated, all were aware of a tall, sinister-looking individual standing beside Patrick. Slowly this person boldly moved around the outside of the circle. Sago looked human, but he was hissing.

The hissing became louder, emitting a foreboding with each tone. Shamar now understood the tone he was earlier searching for. It was this moment, and it was here that he must take a stand. Shamar understood from the message he received in the secret room that somewhere in him would be the power to defend and protect. Leisurely, Sago paused behind those forced into his submission. However, when he approached Shamar and Eli, he became uneasy and ceased the hissing.

Shamar could feel movement in his lower legs. Was his ability to move returning? Shamar waited a moment more. He was sizing up his enemy, preparing to attack.

Sago stood between Eli and Shamar and began to choke as he tried to hiss behind these individuals.

The Thirteenth Stone of Aaron

Patrick became alarmed as he watched what was happening. He had been promised that nothing would happen to anyone and that all they needed to do was take the treasures and leave. Patrick was aware that Sago's powers were diminished when he was close to Eli or Shamar.

Sago was prompted to slither swiftly away from Eli and Patrick, acknowledging that he would not agitate or challenge these individuals, not yet. Sago's appearance was frightening, and he most effectively exuded an offensive smell that was overpowering, adding to everyone's fright and nausea.

Sago continued to circle each individual to demonstrate his contempt and power over those in the circle. Nevertheless, he remained cautious of Shamar and Eli. He wanted to harm them but was unwilling to challenge their powers—at least not yet. Shamar showed signs of faintness, and he looked nauseous.

Sago continued with a purposeful slow movement, gliding around the circle; however, this time he allowed his long arms to taunt Sophia. Theon recognized this ritual and knew he had chosen his victim.

While Shamar was considering what to do, Sago wrapped his cloak and body around Sophia, drawing her closer to his chest while pinning her arms at her side. Sophia, weak from the mist, was unable to fight back.

Mariah watched, horrified at what was transpiring. A second green mist fluttered down over everyone. This mist was intended to extend the paralyzing effect upon everyone, with the addition of blurred vision. Sago said to Sophia, "Don't worry, my dear, everything will be all right. I will always take very good care of you."

Sophia felt panic building up as she tried to think of how to escape.

Shamar held his breath and quickly made his move toward Sago.

Shocked at Shamar's actions, Sago released Sophia and stepped back a few steps. He was waiting for the fog to paralyze Shamar again.

Shamar grabbed Sago and began to beat on him. Sago, possessing more physical strength than Shamar anticipated, took hold of Shamar's arm, twisted him around, and shoved him down to the floor.

When Sago took hold of Shamar's robe, he cried out in pain and agony. Shamar noticed the burns upon Sago's hands and knew the likelihood of him grabbing his robe again were slim.

After Patrick heard Sago's words to Sophia, he felt anger and betrayal. He quickly ran to the aid of Sophia and wanted to help Shamar.

When Sago tried to stop Patrick from helping Sophia, Patrick plunged a knife deep into Sago's chest. Sago was a surprised by Patrick's actions but quickly backhanded Patrick, which sent Patrick's body sailing down the hallway, landing at its end. Shamar did not falter; he got back up from the floor and continued his assault on Sago.

Within moments, Patrick was running with a renewed strength back toward Sago, who tossed Shamar aside. Patrick was charging and yelling, desperate to free Sophia. Patrick was within striking distance of Sago and yelled, "No, Sago, she is not going to be your toy. This is not what we agreed to." With a powerful thrust, Patrick shoved his pocketknife into Sago's abdomen.

Sago gave a cry of pain and anger.

Everyone had heard the agonizing hiss as Sago was struck by Patrick's knife. Next they heard a disgusting hissing sound, followed by a piercing snap. Patrick screamed in agony and retreated into a corner away from everybody. While running away from Sago, Patrick emitted a strange, unearthly cry of pain.

Shamar paused for a moment. The last assault from Sago had left him dizzy and disoriented.

Sago, this time without a thought for Sophia's feelings, harshly pulled Sophia back into his arms. Sago returned his glance to Patrick, waiting for Patrick to acknowledge who was master. Slowly Patrick turned to face Sophia and Sago.

Sophia noticed the huge wound upon Patrick's face. The wound encompassed his forehead and his entire left eye. Large amounts of blood flowed to the floor.

Patrick whimpered and appeared unsteady on his feet, still wobbling while trying to maintain his composure. Patrick said, "I'm sorry, Sophia. I have failed to rescue you and myself." Unable to stand any longer, Patrick slowly dropped on his knees to the floor. He said again, "I'm so sorry, Sophia. Please forgive me." Patrick slumped over on the floor and did not move again.

Everyone in the room was traumatized by what had transpired and frustrated because they remained in a daze, immobile, with blurred vision, and unable to speak. All they could do was watch and listen.

Sophia realized her body was now totally encircled by Sago. She was on the verge of panic when she felt the cold breeze. She understood Sago was taking her somewhere.

Next she felt the spinning, and Sago clinging around her, giving her warmth from the very cold and dark atmosphere. She saw Shamar; he too was wobbly from his brief encounter with Sago. Her parents, still frozen by the fog, were unable to move to her aid. As the spinning intensified, Sophia succumbed to sleep.

Sometime after Sago's departure, everyone was slowly and independently released from the effects of the fog. Mariah was in tears and screaming at everyone to do something to help Sophia.

Shamar, in a very heartbreaking voice, looked to Theon and Addison, asking, "What can we do? Is there anything we can do?"

Theon was afraid that Eli and Mariah would try to rescue Sophia and that their attempt would be fruitlTheon responded, "Eli and Mariah, I know what I am about to say to you will seem cruel and even pierce your hearts, and you may think I have no feelings or understanding for what just transpired, but please hear me out.

"We have witnessed a small sampling of evil's powers. This was a lower-level evil who answers to a hierarchy that wishes to destroy the good in humanity and rule over them. Sago took Sophia to ensure that none of us would do anything to continue our quest but rather try to rescue Sophia. Yes, we are facing combat in the arenas of good versus evil, and we must prevail.

"As the rabbi stated, this evil intends to rule over good. I'm sure Sago's plan is for us to attempt to follow him so that when we do, others who are more powerful will eliminate us, either individually or as a group. Then they will kill Sophia because she is no longer needed."

Hesitating for a moment, Theon considered his words carefully. "All of us must begin our work to defeat this evil. Eli, Mariah, and Gabriel, the three of you need to return to the cabin and work on the rabbi's correspondence to find any other clues. Also, I need you to research the rabbi and everyone else who assisted Edward.

"Shamar, Addison, and I will return to Alexandria to research what we must do to defeat what we just encountered. We must learn his strengths and weaknesses and who he answers to. This research we are going to do will help us learn where it resides and how we can rescue Sophia.

"This is a very hard concept and difficult request for all of us to consider. However, it is necessary to be successful in rescuing Sophia and completing the quest. I do not believe they will harm Sophia but will use her as bait to lure us in. You cannot fall into their trap, Eli and Mariah. If you want to be successful in rescuing Sophia, we need the knowledge to do so.

"I wish to point out that Sago appeared to be frightened of Shamar. Also Patrick distracted Sago, and in distracting Sago, he kept him from the items he came to take as his treasures. Perhaps Sago will send another creature in his place for the items, especially since Sago was wounded, so we must leave quickly."

Turning to Shamar, Theon looked into his eyes and gently said, "Shamar, I am very sorry for what happened, but if we are diligent in our efforts to learn and understand how we can defeat our enemy, we can and will be victorious."

Addison was crying in the corner of the room. He had gone to Patrick's side, wanting to give him aid, and realized that Patrick had passed away, most likely from a loss of blood by the wound inflicted upon his face. Theon and Shamar went to Addison's side to comfort him. Theon closed Patrick's eyes.

Eli and Mariah were very upset and did not want to leave their daughter with Sago, even if going after her meant they would be harmed. They told everyone that they wanted to search for their daughter.

Theon walked to each of them, and while facing them, he said in a caring manner, "Where are you going to look? And do both of you think you can defeat this lesser evil that we just encountered? How are you going to accomplish your defeat of evil when you don't know or understand what has captured your daughter?

"I understand your emotions of wanting to protect and rescue her, but you are both unprepared, and allowing your emotions to rule your thinking will subject each of you to the evil one's intent to divide and conquer his enemies.

"You must get back to the cabin and find answers. Knowledge is our best weapon, and we do not yet have it."

Gabriel was shocked when he saw Patrick's face. He turned to Addison and said, "You need to know that some men—well, a number of men—are in the process of entering Patrick's mansion as we speak. I noticed them on the monitor when I checked to make sure the door to the bunker was locked."

In an excited voice, Addison said, "Oh my, I believe I know what they are hunting for. They are searching for the key to enter the bunker, and as Theon said, they are here to secure the crate and flasks. We must leave to the secret room *now*."

Eli and Mariah had been talking, and Mariah had difficulty just thinking about leaving her daughter. They decided Theon was correct—that knowledge and strength of numbers would be a better weapon. Eli repeated that they needed to go to the cabin and research so they could come back prepared for what they needed to face and to rescue Sophia.

Mariah grudgingly agreed to Eli's proposal but informed him she was distressed with the situation and concerned over their chances for success. She felt anguished at leaving Sophia's life in the balance while they learned the theory of fighting evil.

Eli placed his hands on each of Mariah's shoulders, and while looking deep into her eyes, he said, "We know what must be done and have a small glimpse of what we are up against; I agree with Gabriel that we must hurry and leave now. The sooner we leave and apply ourselves in the pursuit of knowledge, the nearer we are to rescuing Sophia."

Theon said to Eli, "Now is the time to use the prayer spell in your matchbox. Gabriel, you should be on one side of Eli, and Mariah, you should be on the other. Mariah, you need to read the prayer. Gabriel, the trip is somewhat fast but scary the first time. Please remain in the cabin only, and we will keep in touch with all of you. I would also suggest that if you need any food supplies, place some in the backpacks in this storage room and take them with you."

Gabriel said, "I'll get the backpacks and some food. We can wear the backpacks while we travel."

Shamar asked Theon what they should do with Patrick's body. Theon suggested that they place him on the bed in one of the bedrooms. Shamar and Theon took care of this task.

Addison grabbed the leather backpack, placing it on his back, and firmly adjusted all straps for the travel to Alexandria. Eli, Mariah, and Gabriel followed Addison to the secret room. Gabriel assisted Mariah in adjusting her backpack and asked Eli if he needed assistance.

Theon turned to face Eli and Mariah and said, "I am distressed that Sophia was captured and vow to diligently work to find her captor and to do everything possible to save her."

Theon stepped back, bid the three of them good luck, and once again said, "Stay inside the cabin, and we will keep in touch with you. If you need to contact us, use the robe."

The three gathered together, and Mariah read the prayer. Within moments, they were gone.

Theon did not believe any harm would come to Sophia because of the evil one's desire to obtain the artifacts they had. He knew if his daughter were captured, he too would want to immediately rescue her. He considered the tremendous amount of restraint each displayed in a decision that was difficult. He was grateful all of them had agreed to go to the cabin and complete the necessary research.

Theon glanced over at Shamar and Addison. Softly he said, "Gentlemen, it is time to travel back to Alexandria."

Shamar said, "Please wait a moment, Theon. I think we also need to take some food with us to Alexandria. However, I believe we will need a footlocker full of items."

Addison went with Shamar to the food-storage area. Together they filled one footlocker with military-style rations and a second with water. Shamar took duct tape and wrapped the footlockers securely together for the trip.

Shamar said they needed to travel from where they stood because the footlockers were too heavy to carry. Next he instructed Theon and Addison to sit on the footlockers and hold the handles of the footlocker with one hand and hold on to him with the other.

"OK," said Shamar, "we are ready to travel."

Theon was not too comfortable with the new travel arrangements, but he knew the items in the footlockers were necessary. Theon began to read the prayer. Within moments they began the process of traveling back to their desired destination: Alexandria, Egypt.

Postscript

While some of the concepts in this story may seem outlandish, the artifacts presented in this book have some basis in historical documentation.

Ptolemy Philopater of Alexandria, Egypt, had two secret rooms constructed and hidden within the great Library of Alexandria—one for himself and the second for Alexander the Great.

Theon was the last caretaker of the Library of Alexandria, a counselor to the Roman presence, and a teacher of astronomy, mathematics, and science.

Alexander the Great took a special stone from the Persian treasure room after conquering Persia. He listened to rumors of the stone's purported abilities spewed by a priest and chose to carry the stone around with him. While wearing the stone and wounded on the battlefield, Alexander made a miraculous recovery. His generals made note of his recovery and referred to the stone as the stone of mystery.

When Alexander returned to Persia, he confronted the priest and inquired as to what other abilities this stone was said to possess. Alexander was given a scroll that was thought to hold this information. Fearful that the stone might be stolen, Alexander sent it and the scroll to the Library of Alexandria for safekeeping.

Aristotle received and hid treasures sent by Alexander the Great in a secret location within the library. Upon hearing of Alexander's death, Aristotle packed some treasure in a cart and left Alexandria. Aristotle did not take his beloved books, and he took very few personal items. He was only interested in collecting specific items of Alexander's vast treasures.

After Alexander's death, Persian priests wanted to recover the stone and scroll given to Alexander, since they considered the stone to be theirs. The search began with help from assassins for the stone and scroll.

Made in the USA
Charleston, SC
21 April 2014